THE STORY COLLECTOR'S ALMANAC

MAPPING THE MIST

E.S. BARRISON

Dedicated to Grandma Rhoda & Grandpa David

I think you would both love Malaika.

I wish you were here to meet her.

To Kaina
Knoll
Hutch's Creek
To Heims Norte
Newbird's Arm
The Capitol
Maedee's Outlook
Ab Aeterno
Grover's Marsh
Opal's Canyon
Stilette
To Rosada
To Heims Sur
To Volfium
To Proveniro
To Perennes
Janis

See a more detailed map in the back of the book.

The Council of Mist Keepers

NINGURSU
The God of Death

AELIA
The Healer

TOMAS
The Peacemaker

JULIETTA
The Painter

JIANG
Null

MALAIKA
The Cartographer

ALOJZY
The Architect

CAROLINE
The Illusionist

BRENT
The Story Collector

AL•MA•NAC

a publication containing astronomical or meteorological in-formation, as future positions of celestial objects, star magnitudes, and culmination dates of constellations.

FOREWARD

Not every story has a dark beginning.

Some begin with a flicker of light.

Those are the stories that keep the world beating.

And why I'll continue to tell these tales even when all seems lost.

Over the years, I've collected a series of misfortunes. Death has threatened me on countless occasions, stringing me in the air by tendrils of smoke while threatening to take my mind. It is hard, sometimes, to find the light in this darkness, and even more difficult, it is harder to find people who I can trust.

Especially within the Council of Mist Keepers.

When I first met my teacher, Caroline, and she introduced me to the world of the Mist Keepers, I truly believed I had found the place where I belonged. Little did I know, almost every single Mist Keeper nurtured their secrets in a way that threatened not only my life but the world.

Only one person ever held her truth out to me, wearing it with pride and a grin on her face: Malaika Nuru Jelani.

While Malaika wanders the world as if lost, she has saved me on more than one occasion with her insight. Without question, she is a good person, something that most Mist Keepers lack in constructing their god complexes. She has not abandoned what she loves, and that is admirable.

With darkness and smoke a constant force across the world, it is easy to forget there is good in the world. But Malaika always enters a room with a smile on her face that promises that things will get better.

This is something the world needs.

I know this better than anyone.

Because I am the Story Collector.

And I will keep searching for happy endings.

-*Brenton Rob Harley*
Ninth Member of the Council of Mist Keepers
The Story Collector

ONE

Malaika climbed to the roof to watch the sunrise while her older brother slept, counting as the last stars set behind the horizon. There, she watched as the flittering lizards disappeared into the trees and the drakes wandered back to their caves. Her heart, as always, landed on her family's dragon, Pam, as she paced in her enclosure.

The dragon's obsidian scales cast rays of fool's gold across the air. Around Malaika's neck, she bore one of the dragon's scales. She held it to the light and grinned. People came from all over Leega to visit Ol' Pam—and someday, Malaika hoped, she would ride that dragon across the sky, so everyone could see her glory.

Once the sun passed the trees, Malaika hurried from the roof, nearly toppling into her older brother as he stepped out of the bedroom.

"Watch where you're going," he grunted.

"Sorry, Joshi. Was gonna go help Papa with Ol' Pam."

"Don't think so. Papa's got some visitors today—you gotta stay here with Mama."

"What about you?"

"Papa's showing me the ropes of everything, so I gotta go with him."

"Can't I come?"

"You can't."

"Why? 'Cause I'm a girl?"

"No, 'cause you're a child."

"I'm sixteen!"

"And I'm eighteen, so this farm is gonna be mine someday. And you'll marry some nice man from town, and everything will be all okay." Joshi patted Malaika's head. "Now go comb your hair and help Mama."

Malaika scowled to herself and pulled on a few of her curls before letting them bounce back into place. *My hair is fine. We're not kids anymore.* When she was a child, Joshi used to chase her with a razor, threatening to cut her curls. Only when he ended up cutting his own hand did their parents finally hide all the blades.

She retired to her room to change out of her night-gown, then tiptoed down the stairs to the kitchen. Her mama sat at the table, sorting through a collection of dragon eggs, while Joshi pulled his boots on by the front door. Malaika glowered again in his direction as she sat down with her mother at the table.

"Pam laid three eggs last night," her mama said with a grin. "Didn't think the ol' girl had it in her."

"I think Pam's got a few years left in her." Malaika took one of the eggs from her mother and stared at its scaled shell. "Shame they don't have any life to them."

Joshi interjected as he opened the front door, "We don't go having these eggs to breed dragons. They're what fetch us money so we can live like we do."

"I know that, Joshi!" Malaika barked.

"Yeah, doubt it."

"I know things!"

Joshi chuckled as he left, the door swinging behind him.

Malaika crossed her arms and sank into the chair. Her upper lip twitched.

Her mama placed the eggs to the side and took Malaika's hand. "Don't let your brother get to you, alright, girly? He's trying to get you steaming."

"He doesn't get me steaming!"

"Oh?"

Malaika sank deeper into the chair, frowning more.

"You and Joshi never got along. I know he can be—"

"A self-righteous prick?"

"I was going to say a handful."

"That's a mild way to put it."

Her mama laughed. "I suppose it is. But you can be the better person and not play into his games."

"But it's not fair, Mama! All my life, I've helped around the farm and behaved, but Joshi gets to inherit the farm. He just messes things up!" Malaika argued.

"Once you marry, you'll have to move, Malaika. You know that."

"I told you before, I'm not marrying!"

"You just haven't met the right man—"

"I don't like no one!"

"That'll change, girly. Trust me. I was like you once... until I met Abedi."

Malaika groaned. She'd heard her mother's story plenty about how she fell in love. It didn't encourage Malaika to be excited about marriage. Rather, she squirmed at the thought of marrying any man in her town of Emrys. After being taken from her home, she would become the woman of some house, surrounded by her own children.

It contradicted everything Malaika had ever imagined.

She wanted to fly like Ol' Pam. Was that so hard to believe? Was that such a ridiculous dream?

Her mama smiled at Malaika, then placed the three dragon eggs on the table. She rose and approached the window, staring out at the farm before them. Neither she nor Malaika spoke, letting the silence sift through the air.

Then, her mama exclaimed, "Oh! I forgot!"

"Hm?"

"Joshi's supposed to sheer the sheep this afternoon...and I planned to weave new balls of yarn once the wool is clean. But I forgot to pick up the dyes from town yesterday. I'll have to go there unless—"

"I can go for you, Mama." Malaika jumped to her feet. The idea of getting out of the house held more appeal than anything.

"Are you sure, Malaika? You don't want to help clean the dragon eggs?"

"No, I can go, really!"

"You won't get lost?"

"That was only..." Malaika counted on her fingers. "Four times. Please, Mama? I'll make sure I don't get lost!"

"Okay. But be back by sunset, okay? Don't need your father knowing you were out there. Understood?"

Malaika grinned and said, "I completely understand, Mama."

TWO

As Malaika promised, she traveled into town without getting lost. She ignored the courting of a few men in town, stopping by the local artisan shop to pick up the dyes. With bottles of blue, red, and yellow in her bag, she hurried back from town, taking no time to make small talk. She just had to keep on the path back home, and her father would never know she had left.

"Straight on the path. No turns. Don't get distracted." Malaika recited to herself as she hopped over a couple stones. It was so easy to get sidetracked by the different features of the forest lining the path. While her home country of Leega enamored itself with grassy plains, her papa had traded over the years for countless unique items. Baobab trees from Yilk, black and white patterned flowers from Evylain, camellia bushes from her papa's family in Gonvernnes, and of course, dragons from Spinoza. People from across the country came to their farm to marvel at it.

Even after growing up on it, Malaika still found hidden secrets along each acre. But she had to stay focused. Now was not the time to get distracted.

She had to get home before her papa and Joshi—
She froze.

Just down the path, her papa and Joshi stood with a couple traders, arms crossed, heads together in negotiations. No one saw Malaika, and with dexterity, she vanished into the surrounding trees.

As she snuck through the trees, she kept her eyes on the path. The mere waving of branches or the snapping of twigs distracted her. *Don't get lost. Stay focused. Don't get lost.* Malaika reminded herself every few steps as her papa's voice worked its way through the trees.

At first, hidden, she moved closer until finding a hiding spot a few paces away from them.

"Three for one? What wool are you pulling over my eyes, Monsieur Beaufort?" Her papa asked.

"No wool, Meneer Jelani. No wool at all. You will have three new babes to produce all the eggs, and we'll take the girl off your hands. I think that is a fair deal for us both," Monsieur Beaufort remarked, his hands wrung behind his back. "My partner here, Monsieur Dubois, could bring them by in the next fortnight if you so desire. Or, you can get your pick if you come with us to Château de'la Bêtefumée."

Malaika eyed her papa, rubbing his graying beard and scowling to himself. "She might not be agreeable to this exchange."

Does he want me to marry one of those old mutts? Malaika clenched her hands.

"We can tame any beast, Meneer Jelani. We are not worried about a stubborn pute."

Her papa continued to rub his beard, exchanging a glance with Joshi. Her foolish brother looked on, a smirk on his ridiculous face. *Oh, I am sure he is excited to get rid of me!* Malaika eyed the two men again. If she had to marry one of them, Monsieur Dubois was the younger, far cleaner looking of the two... but not by much. Even from where she stood, Malaika could tell the two men both wreaked of manure and sweat.

"Papa, I can go with them and choose the best of the hatching," Joshi remarked, standing up tall as he finished his sentence.

"Joshi, I appreciate the offer, but I fear you are too green. You gotta have some more experience dealing with men like these."

A scowl crossed Joshi's face. Malaika covered her mouth to restrain her own laughter.

Her papa finally spoke. "I shall leave with you in the morning to observe the stock. I must tell Ayanna, though. She will not be happy about this arrangement."

What about me? This is my life! Tears filled Malaika's eyes. Why did her father never care about what *she* thought? Shouldn't she have a say in her own marriage?

"Until then, I offer you a room for the night," her papa continued, "we would be honored to have men of such high regard staying with us. It will give you time to get familiar with her as well."

"Very good. We appreciate this," Monsieur Beaufort replied, placing a hand on her papa's shoulder.

The group of men walked away, leaving Malaika shaking in her hiding spot. How dare her father give her away like *livestock?* It had to be her they were talking about—no one else made sense. It wasn't like they were giving away her mother or any of the animals. They were worth far too much!

No, she was always going to be the outlier in the family.

"Well," Malaika grunted to herself, "I'm not gonna let 'em get rid of me so easily."

She glanced back into the forest, then smirked.

No. She knew exactly what would get these men running.

Just like all the rest.

THREE

As a child, Malaika pretended she was Uzyma of the Forest. Garnished in roots, leaves, and moss, she ruled the forest with confidence and guile. And now, she returned to Uzyma, blending clumps of mud into her skin, then sticking the brightest leaves on her skin. She wove sticks into her hair, using her curls to keep them sticking out at all angles. Finally, she grabbed clumps of moss, forcing their dirty roots to latch onto pieces of her colorful dress.

If they want to marry me, they have to accept me in full. Malaika laughed to herself, kicking off her shoes so her feet could immerse themselves in the mud.

Every night, her mama used to tell her stories of Uzyma of the Forest, Kifo Kibaya of the Smoke, Asani Azzan of the Flame, Ambar of the Sky, and Nea Reth of the Ocean. She would act out the scenes with Malaika's yarn dolls before leaving her to dream of the tales. Malaika loved the stories, especially those of Uzyma and Kifo Kabaya. Uzyma, the queen of the forest, summoned green with a wave of her hand. Then Kifo Kabaya came to help, tall and proud, kindness as his virtue. Joshi thought the stories silly, but Malaika held to every word, imagining the adventures she might go on if she were like those deities.

The closest she could get was dressing as Uzyma. And now, she could only pray that Uzyma might protect her from a life with those men. After all, Uzyma controlled her life with the magic of the earth in her heart, moving mountains and commanding forests. Uzyma never got lost; she always led with no fear or apprehension.

So Malaika would do the same.

At least once she found her way home.

After sticking the last few branches on her head, she poked her head out of the forest and glanced down the path. With the sun turning orange, the farm took on a life of its own, glowing with orange and bronze. She loitered along the outskirts of it, searching for her home in the haze. Was she even at the right farm anymore? Many times before, she had wandered deep into the forest only to arrive at the neighboring farmland. Joshi never understood how she easily lost her way. The farms all looked the same from a distance! It was easy to get lost on one—at least until the unique fixtures became obvious.

Upon noticing the large barn beneath a set of baobab trees in the east, Malaika knew she had returned to her family's farm. Just to the west of the barn, sitting against the trees, her home waited for her. Shadows—most likely her father, brother, and the traders—vanished into the doorway.

Malaika snuck along the edge of the farm back home. In the distance, Pam's shadow lurked by the barn, her long head bowed. A puff of smoke escaped her nostrils, coating the field around her in a miasma. Every now and again, she extended her wings but never took flight. The entire time Malaika had known the old dragon, not once had the creature flown. Rather, it loitered in its pasture, feasting on its meals and laying eggs.

Just like her papa wanted.

I wonder if Pam misses flying... Malaika rubbed her hands together. *Imagine how easy flying would make everything.*

Her attention fell back on her home. Her heart thudded with every step, excitement bubbling in her throat. *Be confident, just like Uzyma. You are the forest. You are the earth.*

She opened the door to the house, letting the dim light of the parlor greet her. Her father, brother, and mother sat with the traders in the sitting room.

And as everyone turned to her, she took a dramatic bow,

"Hullo there, my dears! It is I—the pute you have come to tame! Well, catch me now if you can!" Malaika smiled.

Monsieur Beaufort and Monsieur Dubois stared at her.

Her father rose to his feet, eyes bugging from his head. "Malaika! What are you doing!?"

"Just showing who I am, Papa. Can't go wrong with that."

"This is ridiculous!"

"What is ridiculous is you giving me to these mutts without talking to me first! I'm your daughter!"

"Who said anything about giving you to them?"

"I heard you when I was coming back from town—"

Joshi let out a loud guffaw. "You think respectable men like Monsieur Beaufort and Monsieur Dubois want a girl like *you*? Don't be so selfish, girl."

"I heard you—"

"We aren't giving you to them. We're giving them Ol' Pam!"

Malaika froze, blood rushing to her face as a knot formed in her throat. Her head spun. "I... I thought—"

"We'll talk about this horrid act later, Malaika. Now go bathe. You look disgusting." Her father turned back to the traders. "I do apologize for her. She does not represent this family."

Malaika's mother filled the wooden bath outside their home before helping Malaika into the water. In silence, she removed the twigs from Malaika's hair while Malaika stared at her dirt-covered nails. *They're getting rid of Pam. Why? She's a good dragon.* The thought of losing Pam hurt her more than personally being given to the traders. Pam had always been part of the farm; now, she was being sold...and for what? Younger dragons? Other creatures? Something else entirely?

"I told you to go to town and come back—no detours," Malaika's mama finally said as she got the last twig from her hair.

"I wasn't going to...but when I was walking, I nearly ran into Papa and Joshi, so I snuck into the trees. Overheard them and—"

"You jumped to conclusions?"

"I didn't think they'd want to sell Ol' Pam. Papa loves that dragon—" Malaika bit her tongue before finishing the sentence. *More than me.*

"Sometimes, if you love something, you have to let it go."

"But he's not letting Pam go! He's selling her. Will Monsieur Beaufort and Monsieur Dubois even treat her well? What if they slaughter her for meat or for her scales or—"

"Now, Malaika, don't let your imagination run. It will only make your head spin."

"But—"

"It's not worth the energy. Trust me, dear. It's not worth it." Her mama stepped back from the tub. "Dreams, stories...they'll run you in circles 'cause they aren't real. This here, now, in this moment, is real. Remember that, Malaika."

"But there's more than this moment, Mama."

"For some people, but not us. This is our moment now." Her mama placed a towel and a clean set of clothes beside the tub. "Now finish cleaning yourself. Your father will have a word with you later, I am sure."

"Yes, Mama."

Her mother started to leave, then turned. "Where are my dyes, Malaika?"

Malaika flushed. "Oh...um...probably in the forest. I can go get them."

"No. I'll find them myself."

Her mother left, leaving Malaika alone to sink into the water. She let it climb up around her neck, not budging until her skin pruned and the sky turned a murky shade of black.

Once the water grew lukewarm, with dirt congealed on the surface, Malaika finally climbed out of the tub. She dried herself off in haste, then pulled on her nightgown. In the distance, against the glow of the moon, puffs of smoke gathered around Pam's barn.

"Guess we're both stuck, aren't we, Pam? I gotta get married someday 'cause my papa doesn't have any good for me...and now you're getting sent off. Not right, really. I don't think, at least..." She took a step forward, her heart lurching for the dragon. She wanted nothing more than to go visit the creature but knew if she delayed any longer, her father's punishment would be even more unforgiving.

"But that ain't right," Malaika muttered as she turned back to the house. "We got our own stories to live, Pam. I know that."

But where could she freely tell her tale?

Four

Her papa lectured Malaika for a good twenty minutes, ranting about the state of her hair and the inconsiderate attitude that she had displayed. Once he finished, anger thick in his throat, Malaika issued an apology to the traders. She obliged without arguing; her father had never hurt her, but his rage was enough to send her back to her room in tears.

She didn't leave her bed for the rest of the night, staring out at the farm until the early morning, never bothering to sleep. In the early hours, the traders left with her father, stopping once by Pam's enclosure. The dragon's shadow loomed over them. *C'mon, Pam, scare 'em or something. They deserve it.*

But the old dragon merely skulked back to her bed.

Malaika didn't dare say a word as she helped her mother in the kitchen, and for the next few days, she behaved. No questions. No running. Silence.

Alone, she worked on knitting a new shawl for winter.

All the while, her imagination danced over Pam's fate.

Would it have been better if they *were* courting Malaika? After all, at least Malaika could fight. Pam didn't have the means to escape, trapped in a life constructed by humans.

But it wasn't like Malaika could help Pam escape. Even if she found the key to the enclosure, the dragon was still a wild animal. Did Pam even trust Malaika? Would she even take flight?

One wrong move and Malaika would be Pam's next meal.

A week after the ordeal, Joshi arrived home from town with a letter in hand. He waved it in Malaika's face before turning to their mama. "Got a letter from Papa! Must be about the trade."

Joshi and their mama gathered around the table while Malaika stayed by the balls of wool she'd been winding. The breaking of the seal, followed by a momentary breath, held the air in place.

She didn't dare ask what the letter said.

But Joshi answered her wonderment anyway. "Papa's secured the trade. They're gonna be back in soon with a caravan to transport Pam." He turned to face Malaika, smirking. "And maybe your little outburst was for the best—sounds like Papa has also secured you a husband."

Malaika dropped her ball of wool on the floor. "What!?"

"Monsieur Dubois was particularly impressed with your guile."

"I...I'm..." Malaika stammered. "No! I'm not gonna marry him!"

"Malaika, dear," her mama whispered.

"I don't want to marry! I won't let him touch me!"

"Malaika, I spoke with Monsieur Dubois after your outburst. He is quite the kind man—"

"He is twenty years older than me!" Malaika objected. "I will not marry!"

Joshi replied, "If you hadn't acted out, this wouldn't have happened. Monsieur Dubois didn't even know you existed until then."

"No. I refuse!" Tears bubbled in her eyes. Before Joshi or her mama could reply, she bolted outside, not bothering to put on her shoes or coat. Her legs carried her across the farm, stomping out her mother's calls. How could her father do this to her? She'd made a point to show her disgust for the two traders! Just like Pam, he was going to send her away.

Pam... She continued racing, heading to where the dragon slept beneath a baobab tree. Malaika paused at the fencing, gripping the splintering wood. What options did she have? They would haul away her and Pam in some caravan, take them far from home. Sure, she always dreamt of adventure...but on her own terms.

By her own flight.

"Pam," she murmured.

The dragon raised her head. With obsidian scales flaking from the dragon's body and deep gray eyes that no longer shimmered like gems, the dragon's age seemed even more pronounced in the sunlight. The creature's wings stretched out once, batted the air, then fell again.

"C'mon, Pam...I know you can fly. If you fly, then at least one of us can get out of here. Because those men are going to take you away...and I dunno what they're gonna do to you. Y'hear me? You can go. I can't...but you can."

The dragon stared at Malaika.

Malaika bowed her head, catching another tear on the tip of her nose. "I wish I could do something, Pam...really..."

Another bat of the wings, but still, the dragon did not lift from the ground. Malaika sulked around the fence, praying to Ambar of the Sky that Pam might just take flight. But the dragon didn't move, only sending bouts of dust into the air and nothing more.

Malaika stared at the locked gate. With three separate locks, it was impossible to break open, preventing Pam from escaping to the forest.

I should run into the forest, disappear before Joshi or Mama find me...

But how long would that last? The town would search for her; people throughout Leega would whisper her name. The only way to be free was to leave—leave Emrys, leave Leega, and disappear into the smoke.

"Malaika!"

She didn't turn.

Her mother ran up beside her, feet equally bare, sweat pricking her hairline. "Malaika..." she breathed.

Malaika said nothing.

"I know that this is not ideal...but think about it! You'll get to travel to Spinoza, live in a new town—"

"And carry the children of a man I don't even know? No, Mama. I'm not gonna do that."

"Malaika..."

"Papa has only ever seen me as dispensable. Guess I'll be out of his hair, though."

"Malaika, no. This is for your benefit."

"No, it isn't." Malaika seethed. "You can lie to yourself all you want, Mama...but don't lie to me. It ain't for the best of nothing. Papa's just getting some new dragons or something out of it...and he's ridding himself of me."

She didn't let her mother respond, turning away again to storm back towards their house.

FIVE

Thoughts of flight haunted Malaika well into the evening. She didn't eat. She didn't speak. She only sat in silence, staring out across the farmland where Pam slept. Every part of her said to run; her father had no use for her, and her mother certainly would not come to her rescue. And, of course, there was Joshi, who taunted her whenever she dared step outside of her bedroom.

Where could she go? What could she do?

She had never felt so trapped.

Until there came a knock.

She'd been sitting by the window for hours. At first, she didn't respond to the knock, but it clanked again like metal falling against the ground.

She hoisted herself from the bed and strolled over to the door. The light of the moon followed behind her, and upon opening the door, it trickled into the hallway.

A set of rusted keys sat on the ground by the doorway.

She glanced down the hallway once, then lifted the keys from the ground. Did her mama leave these here? It must have been her!

Malaika stared at the keys for a moment, analyzing their teeth and rings. Rusted from years of wear, she recognized them. Her father wore these keys on his hip, carrying them out to the farm, opening and closing gates like a guard or a king.

One of these will open Pam's gate! Restraining her laughter, she shoved the keys into her gown. There wasn't a moment to lose!

Without bothering to dress, she hurried down the stairs, tiptoeing over the creaking wood and holding her breath as she passed her mother's room.

In the kitchen, she yanked on her shoes, then rushed outside into the brittle autumn air. She regretted not grabbing her coat at once, but she hadn't the time to turn back to the house. Her heart, her soul, her freedom—it all rested on Pam. If she released the dragon, certainly her own fate didn't rest in the hands of a couple of old men.

The nighttime air made her head spin, but she continued forward, focusing on the barn's shadow in the distance. *Don't get sidetracked. Keep going straight. One step at a time. Keep forward; you're helping Pam.*

She kept reaching for the keys, tracing the different fixtures like Uzyma's gems. These keys belonged to the earth, and with them, she would give Pam back her life.

The gate creaked against the wind as she approached it. Rusted, like the keys, it seemed even larger than it had earlier that day. Malaika held the keys up against the lock, checking each one against it.

After fidgeting with each of the three locks, the mechanism finally clicked, and the gate swung open with a horrendous shriek.

Malaika winced and glanced at the house. No light shone from the windows.

And with that reassurance, she stepped into the enclosure.

Pam slept against the trunks of three old baobab trees. The invasive trees towered over the rest of the forest. They thrived against the heated enclosure, with Pam's warm belly creating a permanent summer climate around her.

Malaika approached the beast. "Heya, Pam. How's it going, girl?"

The dragon opened her gray eyes.

"Look here—the gate's open. You can get outta here and be free. Go on!" Malaika motioned to the gate.

The dragon snorted, then lowered her head to the ground.

"C'mon! Don't be a fool now! You can run! Fly! Be free!" Malaika waved at the gate again. "C'mon! It ain't worth sitting around here and waiting for your fate."

The dragon huffed again. With a loud grunt, she rose from her spot and turned away from her.
Malaika wanted to scream. Why wouldn't the dragon listen to her? Didn't she want freedom?

But as the dragon lowered her body to the ground again, Malaika's frustration vanished, replaced with a deep-seated heartache.

She had never been so close to the creature before, usually watching from afar. But now, in the dim moonlight, she could see why Pam never took flight. A comprehensive lock and chain laced its way across the dragon's back, clipping her wings into place. The chain worked its way down Pam's tail and into a stake deep in the ground, barring her to the enclosure.

"I didn't know... I'm sorry, Pam. Papa never let me so close." Malaika held her hand out to the dragon again. The creature's warmth pounded like a fire.

The dragon did not turn.

Malaika froze. This couldn't be it, right? Pam had to get out of there before Monsieur Beaufort and Monsieur Dubois returned.

She fidgeted with the keys in her hands. *Wait! Of course!*

With another step closer to the dragon, she searched along the keys for one that matched the lock in the center of the dragon's back. Only one bore the right size and shape.

"Heya, Pam...listen here. I'm gonna climb on your back, alright? I think I can get you outta here."

The dragon didn't budge.

Malaika held back her own fear as she crawled up the dragon's magnificent tail. Its scales pricked at her skin, shimmering beneath the glow of the moon. Malaika made sure not to grip onto any scale too tight, pretending instead that she was a leaf floating in the breeze. If Pam felt her, she didn't react.

Now on the dragon, Malaika saw Pam's body in full. Scars covered her scales while open wounds bled with smoke rather than blood. *Did Papa do this to you?* Malaika didn't want to believe her father mistreated the dragon; as far as she could tell, her papa had always tended his animals with love and care. But perhaps that had all been a guise.

Unless this had happened before Pam ever came to the Jelani Farm in the first place.

Malaika didn't take time to observe each scar, finally reaching the lock on the back of Pam's back. She kept hold of the dragon's back with one hand while, in the other, she inserted the key into the lock.

At first, it wouldn't budge.

Then Malaika tried again, forcing her weight into the lock.

Click.

The lock turned.

And the bolt loosened.

She removed the lock. The chains clattered to the ground.

Everything froze for a moment.

Freedom, after all, came with a momentary pause.

A gasp.

And then a screech.

Upon discovering her chains had fallen, the dragon let out a roar that echoed across the farm and through the trees, sending birds flying into the night sky and small critters scattering.

And Malaika laughed alongside Pam.

"See! Now you can go, Pam! Be free! Go on, go—"

Malaika's voice caught her throat when, beneath her, Pam's body rumbled.

Her wings beat.

And with another roar, she leapt into the air.

Malaika screamed, gripping tight to Pam as she took to the sky.

Higher...

    Higher...

        Higher...

And then they were soaring.

Away from the enclosure...

Past the barn...

Over the house where a single window sat illuminated...

Where Malaika saw her mama watching from the window, smiling.

SIX

They soared.

In the darkness, Malaika hadn't a clue where they were traveling nor the direction they were headed. Even with the moon falling before her, she didn't remember if it rose in the east or the west. The stars held no meaning. By the time the sun started its ascent, the only thing she knew for sure was that she and Pam no longer resided in Leega.

With the sun peaking over the distant mountains, Malaika adjusted herself on Pam's back, gripping tight to the creature's neck. Pam soared with ease, her wings battering behind Malaika. It was nothing different from riding a horse, really. A little bumpy, a tad uncomfortable, but the ride itself was smooth and gorgeous.

Below, baobab trees intermingled with the plains, with not a single cedar or oak tree in sight. Small towns lay dispersed on the ground beneath them, and Malaika swore, as they continued to fly, that people rushed from their houses and pointed to the sky. Wherever they were, dragons were just as much a legend as Uzyma and Kifo Kabaya.

So at least I know we're not flying to Spinoza. Malaika thought as she waved down at a couple of children running from their homes.

Wherever they were heading, Pam moved with determination.

And Malaika wore her happiness with a touch of uncertainty. Only with the rising sun did the gravity of the situation weave its way into her; she was far from home, free from the obligations of her family. But she was alone. She had no money, no food, and no knowledge of the world before her. Her freedom had come at a cost.

But she couldn't assess her future until Pam landed.

She did manage to assemble mere ideas. Water, lodging, food—once she had those, she could then start her new uncertain life. At home, when dreaming about a life of flight, she only saw adventure and excitement. But she had to step back from that, be realistic; she had nothing but the clothes on her back and a dragon to guide her. That would not be enough to support her adventure.

Despite her gnawing exhaustion, her mind continued to race well throughout the day. Pam relished the flying, not seeming to let up, despite the pounding sun or passing clouds. Did she have a destination in mind? Or would she just continue to fly until exhaustion finally seeped into her wings?

The answer came at sundown. It was already a day since Malaika first took flight. Her stomach growled angrily while her head pounded from the hours in the air. She had tried sleeping, but Pam's lurching and breathing woke Malaika from any deep slumber. One of those lurches came as Pam began her descent, matching the cadence of the setting sun.

With the sky surrendering to a purple hue, Pam finally hit the ground.

Malaika clamored from the dragon, her body wobbling as she landed on her feet. They'd landed on an empty plain composed of blackened grass and towering trees. Only the small oasis of water blessed them with reprieve. Malaika raced over at once, cupping water into her mouth before collapsing against a nearby tree.

Where were they?

In the distance, flickering glows of fire called to her. *At least we're close to civilization.* Malaika smiled to herself as she leaned against the tree. Another pang of hunger knocked against her stomach. Once the sun rose, she would search for food. For now, exhaustion was her dearest friend, seeping over her.

And when she next opened her eyes, morning light greeted her with a warm smile while her hunger screamed at her like one of Pam's roars.

She cursed under her breath, rubbed her eyes, then clamored to her feet. Pam rested by the oasis, still fast asleep.

"Heya, Pam," Malaika yawned as she walked over to the dragon. "You hungry, girl? Maybe we ought to find some food. Alright there, Pam?"

The dragon didn't budge.

"Pam, I can't do the hunting for both of us. You eat three times as much. You gotta help a little." Malaika placed a hand on the dragon's body.

Her stomach flipped.

It's cold.

No warmth escaped Pam's skin. Not a breath lingered from her nostrils.

"Pam?" she squeaked.

The dragon did not flinch.

"Pam!?" Malaika screamed, this time rushing to the dragon's face.

The dragon's eyes remained shut, resting in peace.

SEVEN

Malaika wandered away from the oasis in a daze. Had she caused Pam's eternal slumber? Or had the dragon sought out peace on her own accord? Was this her final journey? Had this been what she was waiting for after all this time?

Either way, it didn't matter: Pam was dead, and Malaika was alone.

She wandered with uncertainty towards the city in the distance, flickering like a mirage against the bearing heat of the desert. Like a beacon, its tall, burned tower remained as a constant shadow over the land. Would the people there even speak Leeg? Or would she wander alone, nothing more than a beggar on the street? No... she couldn't think like that. This was just the start of her adventure. She just had to think on her feet, write her own story, and start a new life.

Easy... right?

She hugged herself as she approached the town. A stone archway towered above her, at least three times the height of a normal person. An obscure language dotted the fixture while two floating flames sat on either side of the entrance.

The buildings stood at the same height. Doorways towered. The shortest doorknobs sat at exactly Malaika's height. Even the bricks paving the roadway appeared bigger, extending five footsteps, overshadowing the flowering weeds that nestled between them.

Then there were the people. Malaika ducked into an alley upon seeing the first person. While Malaika barely reached her brother's shoulder, these people made her feel like an insect. They stood at least twice the height of her brother and father, footsteps heavy and moving with a determined stride. *Are these really giants?* she wondered as she watched a mother and child walk past her. The child already loomed over her, still skipping along like any other happy child in the world.

They'll step on me if I'm not careful. Malaika stayed close to the wall as she walked. Surely she couldn't be the only non-giant here! No, there had to be others. This city might have stood alone in the center of the desert, but it had to trade or interact with the rest of the world.

She continued to navigate the city, peaking into any open crevasses and plazas.

A market square sat at the center of town, bustling with people going about their shopping. Malaika tiptoed beneath the vendor stalls. Despite the size of everything else, most unprepared food remained standard in size. It made it easy enough to snatch fruit off one of the stalls, which she devoured in seconds to quell her stomach.

No one noticed her. She was like a shadow.

Or an insect.

Or perhaps a squirrel.

Unnoticed. Unimportant. Unknown.

She didn't even understand what anyone said.

Thoughts of home returned to her, but she shook them away at once. She didn't miss home, per se, but rather comfort. There, at least, she could expect another meal, anticipate a warm bed, and lean into her family's companionship. But even if she wanted to go back to the farm, the question remained: how? She hadn't a clue where she was or how far she had traveled.

"Thanks a lot, Pam," Malaika mumbled as she tossed a pear core at the wall. "You couldn't have waited 'til we found somewhere safe to kick the bucket, huh?"

She imagined Pam huffing at her in distaste. The dragon had all the right to go where she pleased. Malaika hadn't planned to join her.

Malaika only hoped that her mother forgave her for flying off like that.

Unless Mama knew.

She climbed up from the ground and started down the road. She had to be careful to avoid the doors to different homes and shops as she walked. One hit, and she would go toppling.

Despite knowing that, she still almost fell backward as a door squeaked open.

An old man, closer in height to her father than to the giants in the city, peeked out.

He said something in an unfamiliar language.

Malaika stepped back, shaking her head.

The man spoke again, "Sorry there, dear. Imagine you don't speak no Yilkan."

"You speak Leeg?" Malaika asked.

"Yeah, yeah, sorry there. Not used to ones our height coming through." He tilted his head to the side. "What you doing here? You can't be older than fourteen!"

"I'm...I'm eighteen! I just look young. Some...some traders took me from my home, and I escaped."

"I see. I've heard of traders like that before. Ain't good for no one." His gaze softened. "Come. I can make you a hot meal. My wife Tabia will love having a guest."

"Oh, thank you!" Malaika jumped at the idea of a warm meal. "Thank you kindly, Meneer—

"Naidan. But you can call me Jullian. And you're welcome to stay as long as you want."

EIGHT

Jullian and Tabia Naidan welcomed Malaika into their home. Kind folk, who smiled often and shared an undying romance with kisses each night, they treated Malaika as if she were their long-lost daughter, providing well-kept clothing and a bed in which to sleep. The two bubbled with kindness, not just to Malaika but to everyone, it seemed. Jullian was a quiet, lanky fellow with deep-set burgundy eyes and rough hands who sat by the window most days to feed birds or watch the civilians walk past his shop. His wife, Tabia, served a role that Malaika thought only belonged to men: she traded. Her smile reeled in different vendors and customers, bartering to maintain the shop's stock and provide for her family.

It was everything Malaika had ever wanted to become.

Upon arriving, Malaika maintained her lie that she was eighteen. Whether or not they believed her, they never questioned her. They didn't keep her locked away or instruct her when to leave the house. Malaika had free rein to navigate the city and explore on her own according. Armed with Jullian and Tabia's knowledge, the city seemed less ferocious. They told her all about the city: Errat was the oldest city in the country of Yilk, a hub for warriors across the country, as they remained in a permanent battle with the neighboring countries of Sīchóu Shíyóu and Delilah. They detailed the map for her of the city streets and the surrounding countries, but it made Malaika's head spin. She nodded with exuberant interest, then returned to staring at the twisting lines with a pounding headache.

Jullian and Tabia asked her to even show on the map where she was from, but while Malaika knew the country, she could not pinpoint where her home resided. She didn't know if she cared. The more she stayed with Jullian and Tabia, the more she settled into life in Errat. They let her venture as she wanted, get lost in the city for hours, and even let her venture back to the oasis to construct a memorial for Pam. Tabia set her up with a small bedroom and supplied her with wool and needles so she could knit. They only asked that, in return, Malaika helped around the shop—and perhaps knit scarves to give to the soldiers when they visited from the battlefront.

These two strangers welcomed her and treated her like anyone else; sure, they weren't her parents, but at least they accepted her as, well, herself. No one else. Just Malaika.

They taught her how to interact with the giants, as well as how to speak the Yilkan tongue. The giants really did not differ from anyone else, just taller. Malaika had to make her voice a tad louder when speaking to them, of course, but otherwise, it was all the same.

People were people. No matter their height, hair, skin, or talents.

They all came from the same gods.

Yet, what Malaika intrigued the most about Jullian and Tabia was their magic. As a child, she had heard of enchanters and magicians...but she'd never seen them in action. They were nothing but stories whispered by travelers and merchants.

During her first week in their little home, Malaika found Jullian sitting at the table, locked in prayer. When he opened his eyes, he smiled at her and said a hurricane would come in three days, so they must prepare for the winds. Despite no news from any sailors, she helped the old couple board the windows of their home.

And without fail, the hurricane arrived.

"I'm a seer, you see. I can see things coming from the future," Jullian explained as they sat around the fire, waiting for the storm to pass. "The storm will pass tomorrow, then we can go back as we do."

And as he promised, the storm passed.

The next morning, Malaika followed Tabia with glass jugs on her hips. The storm left the road in shambles, with flooding in the street and trees fallen on their sides. Tabia did not seem phased, and she approached the deepening puddle with her jugs, using them to scoop the murky water from the ground. Once filled, Tabia asked Malaika to help bring the jugs inside and place them on the table.

There, Tabia circled them once before tapping on the glass.

The water spun within the container.

Then cleared.

Malaika tried to form a question, but her tongue twisted in awe.

Tabia smiled at Malaika. "Could you help me fetch more water, dear? There are some more containers in the basement. Jullian said the east side of the city experienced some severe damage, so I would like to get this water over there sooner rather than later. Understand?"

Malaika obliged and thus stepped into her new life.

NINE

For three years, Malaika lived life undisturbed with Jullian and Tabia. She continued to help around the house, listening to their stories. The couple had left Leega long ago to make a better life for themselves. With no children or family, they had nothing to lose. In Yilk, they became the masters of magic and vision; everyone trusted them.

But the couple's age proved a detriment. There were days when neither of them got out of bed, or they even forgot Malaika's name. It was a heartbreaking but necessary truth. Malaika had arrived too late to celebrate every facet of their lives.

But they celebrated every moment she stayed beside them. Never once did they ask her to marry or to leave, but to just be there with them.

More and more, Malaika took control of the shop, delivering water to those who needed it and selling convoluted maps to visitors in Errat. All the while, Jullian fretted over the finances, and Tabia kept the house in good order. Malaika never asked about the financial situation. Once she finished the day and closed the shop, she ventured out into the city. She explored every corner, unraveling its secrets before returning to the shop for a warm meal and an intriguing story from Jullian and Tabia's long lives.

Her heart continued to weigh heavier with the passing of the days. The inevitable stalked her. Once Jullian and Tabia died, where would she go? Would she continue to run the general store? What if the finances were worse than she thought? Would she be forced to sell it and flee? Now that she could speak Yilkan to a degree, the city no longer scared her. This was her home.

But perhaps there was more waiting for her.

So she continued, waiting for the inevitable. Not that she feared Kifo Kabaya and the death he brought, but the uncertainty of the future that followed.

One day, as she closed the shop, the door opened with a single chime of the bell. She hardly lifted her head as a giant entered. He strode into the house, weaving his long hair into a ponytail as he glanced around the room.

"Oh, hello!" Malaika said in Yilkan. "We're closing, but if you see anything—"

The man didn't respond, snagging a bottle of wine from a shelf and ripping out the cork with his bare hands.

"Sorry, you need to pay for that."

The man still didn't reply, marching up the stairs towards Jullian and Tabia's room.

"Excuse me! Don't ignore me!" Malaika chased after him.

The man moved fast, taking two steps at a time. The door to the bedroom opened without him even touching the knob. A strange mist bellowed at his feet like shadows. It reminded Malaika of the smoke that used to gather around Pam but more controlled. She hadn't noticed it when he first walked in, but now it filled the stairwell, nearly blinding Malaika.

"You're not allowed up there!" Malaika raced behind the man and into Jullian and Tabia's room.

She froze.

The man was nowhere to be seen. There was nothing but a trail of smoke gathering at the foot of the bed where Tabia sat holding Jullian's frail hand.

"He's gone," Tabia whispered.

"Wha—what?" Malaika stepped back from the door, scanning the room for the man. What had he done? Where had he gone?

"Jullian. He just stopped breathing a few moments ago."

TEN

The gravesite sat on the northern edge of the city, marred by an archway inscribed in Yilkan. Malaika still struggled to read the strange glyphs, but Tabia translated them as they arrived.

"Our sun shines with yellow rays. Join infinity with our sons and daughters," she read.

Malaika nodded once and took the old woman's hand.

They spoke not another word as they entered the gravesite. Only the flickering of the pyre in the center of the yard sang, casting embers into the air in plumes of gentle smoke. Jullian's body lay in the heart of the flame, body succumbing to the heat, withering away like a piece of wood.

Malaika didn't know what to say. Her heart ached at the sight, but she hadn't known Jullian like Tabia. She arrived in their lives as a single guest. Now...they would be a momentary tale in her own existence. A memory—just like Pam and her family. Each moment moved forward like a gust of wind.

A breath of air.

A plume of smoke.

Only to vanish by the morning.

"Did he know Kifo Kibaya was coming?" Malaika finally asked.

"Hm?" Tabia lifted her head.

"He sees things, doesn't he? Did he expect that Kifo Kibaya would come that day?"

"Jullian knew it would be soon. He was ready. Before you showed up, he was ready. It was just a waiting game." Tabia held her hand out over the fire. "He won't be waiting long, though."

"What're you talking about?" Malaika asked the woman.

"Jullian and I have been together since we were sixteen years old. Fell in love, ran away... set up this shop. And the heart knows when it is time." Tabia dropped Malaika's hand. "It has been a pleasure these past couple of years, Malaika. I hope you'll continue your journey with a golden soul."

"What are you talking about, Tabia?"

"Take care, Malaika. We will meet again in Kifo Kiba-ya's realm."

Before Malaika could stop the old woman, she stepped into the flaming pyre.

Malaika screamed.

Yet her shouts did not stop the fire. With the stench of burning leather, Tabia collapsed against him in a single gasp, clothing and hair reduced to embers. Malaika couldn't bring herself to move, locked in a state of shock as the old woman's body continued to perish. What would she tell the customers? What about the undertaker of the graveyard? Would anyone believe her if she told them that Tabia Naidan had burned herself alive?

Frankly, Malaika didn't understand the sacrifice. Even over the years, she hadn't fancied anyone in the slightest. Why give away your life because you lost another?

But hadn't she sacrificed her own life for Pam? Or had Pam sacrificed hers for Malaika?

She wasn't so sure anymore.

Tabia's hand fell to the side, reaching out from the fire, motionless. With tears stinging her eyes, Malaika reached for it; one last goodbye to a friend, a goodbye she hadn't been able to give her mother.

What was her mother up to now? What about her father? What about Joshi? Did they miss her? Did they even think about her?

She'd be lying if she said she spent days thinking of them. They popped into her dreams and flittered through her brain before disappearing in the back of her mind.

Would Jullian and Tabia appear in her dreams the same way now that they had gone?

She reached for Tabia's hand, charred and warmed from the fire.

A momentary spark crossed the tips of her fingers.

And the flames eroded around her.

The fire danced.
And danced.
Mocking.
Screeching.
Laughing.
But they did not scar.
Only chattered.
In their enraged glare, she searched.
For what?
She only saw the fire.
Disoriented.
Lost.

A maze.

An endless path.

Straightening as Malaika walked.

Clearing the path.

A single line on the map.

And before her, someone wandered with the same absent-mindedness.

Nothing.

Wandering.

Then she called out.

The figure turned.

A beat.

Then two.

Tabia stared at Malaika.

"Lost... no Jullian..." Tabia bemoaned.

Malaika motioned Tabia to follow. "This way. From where I came."

"Are you sure?"

"It's a straight line. A single path. Hard to get lost there, huh?"

Tabia nodded once.

And together, they ventured back...

And into the flames.

Malaika pulled away from Tabia's hand. Smoke extended from Tabia's fingertips, wrapping through the air and coming together to form a dense cloud in front of Malaika.

She squinted.

Before her, she swore, Tabia stood. A smile crossed the old woman's face.

"Are you... dead? A ghost?" Malaika asked.

Tabia said nothing, her smile remaining locked in place.

"Does this mean that I'm like Kifo Kibaya?"

Tabia shrugged and, with a smile, disappeared into the mist.

ELEVEN

Malaika moved away from the pyre, her hands shaking at her sides. She still didn't understand what had occurred—was she Kifo Kibaya now? Or was it merely a fluke?

Or perhaps a trick of the light?

She wracked her brain over the stories her mother used to tell her. While she'd committed most of Uzyma's tales to memory, Kifo Kibaya's remained a more distant recollection. How had it gone? She pulled a memory of her mother, sitting by her bed, into the front of her mind.

Her mother told her the story with a smile one evening. "Kifo Kibaya spends his days loitering in the mist, holding a hand to the dead and hoisting them from their nightmares. At his heart, he is a good man, but the mist can be alluring, filled with magic and surprises. It is Uzyma who keeps him from getting lost in its prowess. But do not fear Kifo Kibaya, my dear. He is here to help. As we all try to do. Help."

Malaika stared back into the waning fire. *Is that what I did? Help?*

She opened and closed her hands. Where could she go now? Was she able to go back to their shop alone?

As she turned, a figure entered the gravesite. Hulking like all the other giants, its shadow extended across the ground, grappling toward Malaika's feet. The figure that bore it stood in the gateway, long black hair swaying behind his head, arms crossed over his burly chest.

It's the same man that invaded the shop when Jullian died! Malaika froze in place. Was it Kifo Kibaya? Had he come to release Tabia's soul?

What would he do when he discovered Malaika had already conducted the release?

He didn't move at first, as still as a marble statue. He removed a flask from his hip and took a drink. After swallowing, he blinked a few times, then returned the flask to his side. His eyes latched onto Malaika.

"You again..." he hissed.

"Yeah, came to put Jullian to rest. Tabia decided to join him."

"So it goes," the man replied.

Malaika willed the courage to ask her next question, "Are you Kifo Kibaya?"

"It does not matter," the man said as he stepped towards her.

"I'd say it does. You've popped up twice now after people die!"

"Coincidence. An unfortunate one at that."

"I think you're lying!" Malaika shouted up at the giant, eyes locked with him. He wasn't the tallest giant she had encountered, but he held a presence that filled the gravesite. But Malaika refused to step back from him; if he was Death, she had no reason to fear.

Death came to help.

But doubt fell into her stomach as the man continued to bear down on her. He arched his back, lingering over her with disgust. His breath hit her skin, warm and wreaking of liquor.

Then came his hands, swift like a knife, lacing around her neck.

Malaika went to scream.

The man tightened his grip.

A pause.

A beat.

A thud.

Then a snap.

And nothing more.

TWELVE

No clear paths.
No roads.
No direction.
A wandering soul.
Marching...
Marching...
Marching...
She walked with no destination.
No clue.
No direction.
Where was she now?
Sometimes, in a forest.
Others, in the sea.
Nowhere.
Everywhere.

Lost...

    Lost...

        Lost...

Did it matter? She was free.

Free to be.

To exist.

Lost...

    Lost...

        Lost...

Walk straight. Don't detour.

She recited the words with each passing moment.

Keep focused. Don't delay.

One step...

    Two steps...

        Three...

She strode forward,

Heal to toe.

Imagining a compass,

A map,

Or a guide.

Waiting...

    Loitering...

        Watching...

And with an arm outstretched, she kept her pace.

Did not delay.

Did not detour.

Until the path ended in a bout of light.

THIRTEEN

Malaika jolted awake, sweat marring her brow. Flames rose around her. She yelped at once, jumping out of the fire and landing on the ground of the gravesite.

She blinked a few times as she gathered herself. Sunlight beat from the sky. Against the nearby fence, the undertaker of the gravesite raked away at the surrounding leaves.

"Oh, hullo!" Malaika called to him. "How long have I been out?"

The undertaker did not reply.

"Hullo?" Malaika stepped towards them.

Nothing.

Malaika furrowed her brow, then glanced back behind her. The pyre glowed, and within it, a corpse disintegrated into smoke. Malaika approached it.

Her stomach fell.

Despite the disappearing nature of the corpse, she recognized it at once. She stared down at her fingers, comparing them to the body lying within the flames. The fingernails, the stature, and the curly hair all loaned themselves to one clear truth: *That's me.*

And at the realization, the body vanished like mist, nothing more than ashes in its place.

"What!?" Malaika stumbled backward from the pyre. The undertaker still did not reply. She was there, then she wasn't... and now she stood here, unseen by the undertaker. "What's going on? Where am I?"

She approached the undertaker and waved her hand in his face. Still, he did not turn.

Malaika cursed, and with her heart ringing in her ears, she hurried away from the gravesite, passing under the arch and back into the city. She ran across the cobblestone, her footsteps echoing, but no one noticed her. Even as she darted between two giants, nearly tripping them. While they fumbled, they did not look for the culprit, as if Malaika were nothing more than a ghost.

Was she a ghost? The man, who had to be Kifo Kibaya, snapped her neck. Surely, she shouldn't have survived! Then... did that mean she was dead? But why didn't Kifo Kibaya help her from the torment of her mind? Why did she have to escape alone?

As her mind raced, smoke gathered around her. It moved with her, like a tunnel or a pathway, and guided her through the city—just like Pam did when they escaped the farm.

Am I alone? Dead? What happened?

Would she wander, lost and alone, for eternity? How did the story go again? Uzyma gave life, but Kifo Kibaya helped cross over to eternity, alone, wandering...

Was he lost?

Or just... wandering?

She huffed in frustration, and around her, the smoke dissipated.

And once again, she stood before Jullian and Tabia's shop.

She climbed up the steps and walked inside the building—untouched, empty, and silent. The shop belonged to no one now. Someone else would have to take possession of it, supply goods to visitors, and continue its tale.

Malaika climbed the stairs to the room where she used to stay. Even if she was dead, there was no reason not to take her belongings. She shoveled her clothes into a bag, followed by a rusty compass that she couldn't read and a map that made little sense. Where would she go? What would she do? The walls closed in around her.

"Is this my mind in torment?" Malaika wondered aloud. She had wandered in a nightmarish darkness, but perhaps it was only the beginning of her terror. Had Kifo Kibaya locked her away for good? Had she done something wrong?

"No, you are free," a voice responded.

Malaika glanced into the doorway. A grin crossed her face. "Jullian! Tabia!"

The old couple stood in the door, flickering in and out as if made of smoke or air.

"You are not alone, Malaika. We are here." Tabia knelt beside her.

"Did you follow me from the gravesite? Does this mean I'm dead?"

"No, we knew you would be here." Tabia glanced at her husband.

Jullian added, "As you know, I am a seer."

Malaika nodded.

"I saw a vision of you in this interim world of Life and Death with Tabia and me soon after we first met. I didn't understand what it meant... until I could see my death coming." Jullian grunted as he sat on the cot. "I told Tabia that soon after I passed, she should follow. I watched as you and Tabia brought my body to the graveyard... and I saw you release Tabia from her terrors after she committed to her death."

"Yes, I released her like Kifo Kibaya would. I didn't even know I could."

"Then perhaps it means you are the replacement for Kifo Kibaya?" Jullian asked.

"Y'know, I thought that, but it doesn't make sense. Wouldn't the old Kifo Kibaya teach me something?"

"That is a question I cannot answer, nor can I see an answer. Death took away my sight. The future is as much of a mystery to me as anyone."

"Your magic is gone?" Malaika turned to Tabia. "What about yours?"

Tabia grimaced before saying, "The water does not call for me anymore. I think our magic returned to Uzyma, where it belongs. It was but a temporary blessing."

"So, what does that mean now?"

"It means we are here for you," Tabia said.

"Until it is time for us to move to eternity," Jullian added.

"You mean, you'll stay with me while I figure out whatever is going on with... me?"

"If you wish."

And Malaika did more than wish.

She embraced the elderly ghost couple, her family in the world of mist.

FOURTEEN

Days blended into weeks, and weeks blended into months. Malaika didn't leave the City of Errat, navigating her new role in the afterlife with Jullian's and Tabia's help. Every movement, every decision, came with guesswork. At first, she spent the days wandering the city streets, searching for the dead while acting like Kifo Kibaya. She would let the strange mist lead her toward the gravesites and clinics before returning to the streets. Jullian and Tabia stayed by her side. At night they would gather in the old shop to tell chat and tell stories just like before their deaths, with Malaika knitting, Tabia cooking, and Jullian polishing a pair of shoes.

With death, it was as if the secrets of life vanished. Malaika told Jullian and Tabia the true nature of her arrival. They held no anger, and Jullian nodded as though he already knew.

Malaika wondered how the man might struggle without enhanced sight. Did he wish he envisioned the future now? Or what about Tabia? Did she miss the way water used to sing?

Most of all, Jullian's magic would have been helpful the day the tax collectors arrived to seize the shop.

They marched into the store clad in their suits, eyes darting around the room. One of them knocked over a display.

"Oi! Mr. Naidan—you're overdue again!" the tallest tax collector shouted.

Malaika stood before them, frozen. She still wasn't used to not being *seen*, wrapped instead in a tight grip of the mist of the dead.

"We know how much you like this shop. Don't make us break anything." The other tax collector bellowed as he knocked over another display.

"Stop!" Malaika shouted as she stepped in front of them. She imagined the mist parting, presenting her with a clear path, so they would heed her words and her thoughts.

And the mist, at her own demands, did just that.

"There's money in the drawer! Take that and leave!" She continued.

The tax collectors froze. The tallest one narrowed his eyes in her direction.

"Where'd you come from?" He asked.

"Doesn't matter. Take what we owe you and go." Malaika kept her voice firm.

"You weren't there before!"

"It's 'cause I'm an eerie ghost. So go." Malaika waved her hands at them, then, with the idea of mist shrouding her again, stepped back from them.

The tax collectors gawked between themselves. Then, without bothering to open the door, they fled from the shop.

Malaika placed her hands on her hips and chuckled. "Well, I don't know what I just did, but it seemed to work."

"You're getting used to this mist of the dead," Jullian said as he joined her side. "I wonder if it can guide you forward."

"What do you mean? Like a map?"

"A map. Yes, that's a good explanation." Jullian nodded to himself. "If I could see your future, I might be able to tell you more."

"Then I guess we're gonna figure this out together."

Tabia joined them. "Malaika, we can only guide you so far."

"I'm confused."

"You will have to figure some of this out on your own. Remember, there is much more for you if you are indeed Kifo Kibaya."

Malaika's stomach dropped. "Wait. Are you saying that you are going to leave me? After all of this?"

"No, of course not—"

"Not yet, at least," Jullian added as he took Malaika's hand. "When the time comes, though, you must be ready to be on your own... as that is the future I saw many years ago. Wandering... alone."

"Alone..." Malaika swallowed.

"We'll make sure you are ready. Don't worry."

"But what if I never am?"

"You flew here on a dragon," Jullian said. "I think the world beckons you to wander. It is your calling... and we will help you fly again."

After Jullian and Tabia retired for the evening, Malaika stepped outside, catching the wind in her hair. The mist shifted around her while Jullian's words weighed heavy on her mind. She knew, of course, that Jullian and Tabia would leave someday. But what would she do without them? She was lucky they returned to her in the first place. Otherwise, wouldn't she have spent her time alone, unsure, wandering?

She captured a plume of smoke in her hand and let it dance around her fingers. Without her friends by her side, she would be lost, like a traveler without a map. How would she even know where to go? Pam took her here, far from home, and she still couldn't locate a way back to her farm on the map.

Although, she spent little time looking, either.

"Guide me...please. Show me," Malaika whispered to the mist. She imagined it forming a compass or a clear path just for her. It could lead her to those who needed help and let her wander wherever destiny called.

From what she could gather, the mist was a product of Life and Death, bowing to her every whim. It did not differ from helping a poor soul out of terror and into eternity.

The mist wove around her like strands of yarn. Malaika imagined a pair of needles coming together in her hands and knitting the strands into a complex map-like shawl. With the mere thought and memory of the movement, the mist obeyed.

It spun together, constructing the shawl in Malaika's mind. Yet, it was not a true shawl but rather a detailed work of art, spinning in circles. The wind danced with it, and Malaika's laughter sang alongside it.

And with a gasp, the strands of mist settled, knit together in the shape of the city.

Malaika paced around it, a grin wide on her face. The map came together, a product of her dreams, as a perfect replica of Errat. In a matter of seconds, she had constructed a piece of art. It detailed everything, from the gravesite on the outskirts of the city to the weaving paths and markets and up to the burned tower in the center of the city. She circled it, taking in the details as it floated before her.

She reached forward to touch where the shop sat. At her touch, the map shifted, seeming to focus on that exact piece of the city.

Not only that, but the map also saw the city in that moment.

There she saw, in that image, a miniature version of herself, staring at a tiny map, just as she did.

Malaika waved her arms. The miniature version did the same.

When Malaika jumped in place, the miniature version followed.

And when Malaika laughed, so did the version on the map.

"Oh, this is fantastic!"

She clapped her hands over the map in excitement. The map vanished.

Malaika cursed. She waved her hands over the air again.

The map reappeared.

Another laugh followed.

Oh yes, this was exactly what she wanted.

She couldn't wait to tell Jullian and Tabia.

FIFTEEN

As the resident experts in magic, Jullian and Tabia helped Malaika maintain control over her map. It all came down to focus; Malaika couldn't get distracted. She had to keep the map in the forefront of her mind whenever she used it. They helped her channel her focus on the map, work her energy into the mist, and let her magic take form. It was strange, giving into this world of the dead.

But it was her life now. Or her death. She wasn't sure what to call it anymore.

This map was more than just a guide to the city, though. With a wave of her hand, the map would tell her where a soul needed rescuing. If she spent long nights wandering, getting derailed by the identical roads, she would use the map to check on Jullian and Tabia. Although, she didn't check often, respecting their privacy, and instead used the map to discover every corner of the city.

The once mysterious city of Errat, with its winding roads and towering structures, became Malaika's kingdom. Within the next year, she learned every crevasse, every alleyway, and every corner. Her map grew with her knowledge, able to track movements and sense people on their last breath.

But as Jullian and Tabia had said, they could only teach her so much.

The earth called for Malaika.

And she wanted to wander.

After a year of helping the dead of Errat, Malaika understood it was time. She would return someday, that she promised to herself, but others needed her help in the world. No longer did the city's walls hide her.

With her decision, she packed her bag early one autumn morning, filling it with a change of clothes, some food, haircare supplies, and her knitting needles. Uncertainty chased her movements as she descended the stairs. Where was she going? She hadn't a plan or a clue, only the certainty that she had to take the next step.

When she was younger, she dreamt of this freedom. Now it lay before her, more welcoming than ever.

Jullian and Tabia waited in the shop's entrance for her, smiles on their translucent faces. Malaika didn't know what she would have done without them. But now, they all knew, this part of her journey had ended.

"We are proud of you, Malaika. You've done so well." Tabia placed a hand on Malaika's cheek. "It's been an honor these last couple of years."

"I am going to miss you both." Malaika glanced between Jullian and Tabia. "I don't know what I would've done without you."

"You would have survived—because that is who you are."

"After all, few people can say they rode across a continent on the back of a dragon." Jullian touched her shoulder. "Your family would be proud of what you became."

Malaika's stomach fell. *Family.* She had thought little of them, really, except for the fleeting thought of her mother telling her stories about Uzyma and Kifo Kibaya. Yet, her father and brother rarely crossed her mind. Were they okay? Did they miss her? Did they think she was dead?

Well, then again... she was dead. But that was beside the point.

"You're my family. If I made you proud, then I'm alright." Malaika took both Jullian's and Tabia's hands.

The ghosts grinned back, tears dotting their eyes as they squeezed Malaika's hands.

"What will you do now? Are you... going on to eternity?"

The couple glanced at each other, then shrugged.

"We'll see where our souls lead us," Jullian said. "Perhaps we'll stay here, run a little ghost shop for others passing by."

"Oh, I love that idea, dear!" Tabia remarked.

"Then we can try. It will be our next project."

"So I'll see you again then?" Malaika asked.

"We can only hope."

Malaika embraced the old couple. She promised it would not be the last time.

Malaika took her time reaching the edge of the city. Each step weighed, and while the mist helped her move with speed, she cherished each footstep. With every turn, she said goodbye to the different twists and turns of the city, only pausing to help souls from the terror of death. She stayed close to the mist, rarely appearing to those alive. Why did she spend most of her time hiding in the mist? While it seemed to go with the role, it didn't mean she had to obey it.

But no one is here to tell me what to do. I can come up with my own rules. She smirked as she approached the archway at the front of the city. Who was to stop her from having fun while she helped souls climb to their peaceful eternity?

Alone, with her magic harnessed and the mist as her friend, she could now do whatever she wanted.

She could see the world, chase after dragons, meet new people, and see the magnificence of the world.

At the border of the city, she paused, gazing in the distance at the glistening oasis where Pam had fallen asleep for good. Malaika let the mist guide her there. She had not been there since Pam's death. Something kept her away, her heart heavy, her mind ridden with guilt; she still wondered now what Pam would be doing if Malaika hadn't freed her. Would she still be alive? Or was this the best fate?

Did carrying Malaika cause her pain?

Yet, she could no longer sit with the guilt, and she followed the mist.

With the mist tunneling around her, the trip to the oasis took no time at all. In a mere few moments, she had left behind Errat and the life she had built and stood instead by the water where she and Pam first landed.

There, nothing more than Pam's skull remained, a permanent fixture on the landscape.

Her large nostrils served as a home to a family of rabbits while birds nested between her horns. Moss covered the bone while parts of her once skeletal structure returned to the earth, no remnant of the dragon's grandeur remaining.

Malaika placed her hand on Pam's skull. *Thank you, Pam. Without you, I would never have become... this.*

Her heart lurched. Where would she be now if Pam didn't take her away from home? Married to some trader and stuck on a farm? Would she be a mother to children against her will?

Would she have been happy?

Was she happy now?

The questions weighed, but Malaika knew deep in her core that this was the destiny designed for her.

All because of Pam.

She pressed her lips to Pam's skull. As her lips touched, a spark rose through her skin. Around her, the mist pulled at Pam, like when Malaika released a soul. But something here was different. Malaika couldn't explain it. Rather than a yank and tug with a soul, it was more like a tingling sensation rising through her body.

A sense of emptiness followed.

Then a breath.

As she pulled away from Pam, smoke poured out of the skull's nostrils. It took shape, rising above the oasis. Rather than forming like a soul released from terror, it hovered in the air like a storm cloud, with sprawling wings and a snout-shaped nose.

"Pam?" Malaika called.

The cloud flapped its wings.

Then, with one last beat, it raced across the plains.

Malaika followed.

SIXTEEN

Pam's shadow, as Malaika called it, guided her away from Errat and through the plains of Yilk. As she followed, her map evolved, and every time she called it, new paths and scenes detailed it. In the evenings, when she arrived in different villages, towns, and cities, she would take a room in a tavern and stare at the new intricacies of the map. A few times, she looked back at Errat through the map, taking a chance to peer at Jullian and Tabia. It excited her that the couple had kept with their idea: they continued running their shop in Errat, where ghosts sought goods and conversation.

At first, Malaika kept close to the mist, not revealing herself to the living as she released souls and served her duty as Kifo Kibaya. But even with Pam's shadow riding beside her, loneliness nagged at her. So after wandering alone for a few weeks, with a few ghosts granting her friendship, she dropped her veil. What did it matter if people saw her? She would leave each town in a trail of mist, forgotten by its inhabitants. None of it mattered.

She was just a traveler.

If they didn't forget, then she would just be one of their legends.

A story in her own right.

Besides, no one could tell her what to do otherwise. She was the sole ruler of the mist, the lonely God of Death, the Helper of Souls.

Although, she continued to wonder where that other version of Kifo Kibaya loitered. She had tried to cast him from her mind for over a year, cringing whenever the memory of his hands around her neck returned. The way he stood over her, the glower in his eyes, and the cold touch of his skin would keep her on her toes every passing second. Did that man disappear with her new role? Or was he out there, waiting and judging?

One evening, upon arriving in the city of Tencauri on the border of Yilk and Sīchóu Shíyóu, she took a rest on the lawn outside the historic palace. There, lying in the sun, she recalled the giant again. When she closed her eyes, she envisioned him, with his green eyes cold and scowling mouth marred by an uneven goatee. Her memory kept constructing him in different lights; in one dream, black smoke surrounded him, and in another, beams of light followed his path.

What would Malaika do if he reappeared? He was a giant! She hadn't any skills in combat.

But... she had Pam's shadow...

And her maps.

An idea crossed her mind. She snapped her fingers, and her map formed in front of her. After traveling for weeks upon months, the map had expanded, detailing every place she had ventured and the area just beyond it. Her map had already taken in every nook of Tencauri. She spun her fingers through the map, dissecting its new design. She watched as people strolled in the streets in the northern corner and as children played on a field in the south. The world really was at her fingertips.

She could spy upon anyone.

Watch anyone.

Find anyone.

She paused. *Can I find him? Then I'll always know if he's watching me.*

Malaika expanded the map, focusing on the continent constructed from her travels. Beyond the continent, the unknown lurked in a sea of nothing.

"Show me Kifo Kibaya," she said to the map.

At first, nothing happened. But Malaika kept her focus, just as Jullian and Tabia taught her. She imagined the giant in her mind's eye, focusing on the stories she knew of the Death God. *Show me him.*

The map spun. As it moved, it expanded, beyond where Malaika had ever traveled, east across the sea—or was it west?—to another continent. The land stretched, climbing up a peninsula and into the heart of a forest. There, the map stopped and focused on a swamp blanketed by smoke.

As the smoke parted, a bloodied tree greeted her, arching over where a bearded ghost sat on a stump. He held a round object in his hands. She moved closer to the map to get a better look at the object.

"It's a... head?" She asked aloud.

As if the head heard her, it turned in, staring directly at her.

And the map closed.

"What!?" Malaika waved her hand again. The map reformed, and she immediately traveled back to the swamp.

But this time, the ghost and the head weren't there.

Why did it take me to them when I asked to see Kifo Kibaya? Malaika wondered as she closed the map. There were more secrets hidden in this mist. Alone, she would have to uncover them.

But she could only continue to wander.

Seventeen

With Pam's shadow at her side, Malaika continued her duty—help, explore, and exist. Time meant nothing, and in all honesty, she didn't care. Every location rejuvenated her. From the mountains towering high above Sīchóu Shíyóu to the bouncing waters of the Malva Strait. There, she climbed aboard a boat, hiding behind her own layer of mist, to ride the currents across to the land she had dubbed the Eastern Continent.

Although she might have been heading west.

As she rode the ship, she would let mist take her to islands, freeing souls lodged on their shores, before hopping back to the boat. Pam's shadow rode beside her, diving in and out of the water. No one else ever showed any interest in Pam's shadow; even the dead didn't notice her. But she was always there.

Unless Malaika summoned her map.

Maybe Pam is my map. Malaika realized as the boat docked after many weeks of sailing. She had taken her map out, but Pam did not appear, leaving her alone at the edge of the dock on an unfamiliar continent. She'd grown so used to seeing the giants over in Yilk and even in Sīchóu Shíyóu where their heritage lingered. But now that she had arrived in a small town in the country of Gonvernnes, she was back in a world of people not so tall. Yet, the land remained foreign and obscure. Despite how sometimes she got whiffs of the different languages from releasing souls, this one still couldn't understand the language in Gonvernnes.

I'll get it after a few releases, I'm sure.

She closed her map, taking in the warm summer air with a smile. Pam's shadow reemerged next to her.

"Alright, Pam, let's get going."

"And where are you going?"

Malaika froze. The voice crawled through the air. She didn't dare look.

She knew the voice. Just from one interaction.

It was impossible to forget the voice of her killer.

"I think you're coming with me," he said.

She raised her head, meeting the giant's hard gaze. His scowl and torn cloak stained the backdrop of the pier.

Malaika cursed under her breath. Where could she go? The man held her hostage in his glare.

Trust the mist. She took one step forward, willing Pam's shadow around her. In a gasp, it pushed her forward, sending her rushing past the giant and into the heart of the city. Behind her, in a funnel of wind, another bout of smoke followed. It bellowed and roared as it chased after her, keeping pace as she darted between buildings, trees, and people. The wind knocked a few of them off their feet, but no one saw what had occurred out of sight.

What would they do if they knew two versions of Kifo Kibaya raced in the streets? Would it strike them with fear? Would they bow to them with respect?

She willed her map up as she ran. The man did not appear on her map, but she used it to navigate the winding roads of the port town. Just outside, a forest waited, and there she hoped that the man would abandon his quest.

As she entered the forest, the mist continued to thicken. She pushed it away, only for it to return in heavier force. Even with her map closed and Pam by her side, it did not let up, leaving each tree as a stalking shadow and each turn another mystery.

She circled another tree, tripping over a root and toppling straight into the mist.

Someone caught her.

The hands came first, gripping her shoulders. They didn't consist of the same strength as the giant, holding her upright in place.

Then the mist parted.

Behind it stood a man with a scarred face and sewn closed eye. Sweat dabbed his brow, where a single strand of hair fell between his eyebrows. A shadow weighed over his face.

Then he smiled.

"There you are. Finally."

"What? Who are you? What's going on!?" Malaika pulled away from him.

"My name is Tomás. We've been looking for you."

"We?"

"Ah, yes. You probably do not know anything. I apologize my colleague failed to prepare you properly." Tomás turned his attention to the trees. "Jiang! I found her!"

Malaika stepped back, readying herself to run again.

"Malaika, it is okay. I promise." Tomás said to her.

"Why should I trust you?"

"Honestly, you probably do not have any reason to trust us. Yet, I will tell you that we are fascinated by what you have accomplished. We have never known an untrained Mist Keeper to succeed like you. We are honored to have you amongst our ranks if you choose to join us."

Malaika continued to eye the man, "You best explain yourself. I ain't staying here humoring your or my killer."

"Yes, right. I have heard about what Jiang did to you." Tomás motioned to the tree line. As if on command, the giant emerged, his scowl permanently plastered on his face.

Malaika took another step back from Tomás and the giant. "You have five seconds to start explaining, or I'm gone."

"Yes, Malaika, it is complicated—"

"Three seconds."

"Very well. I'll tell you. Let's go sit. You too, Jiang. We owe her that much."

EIGHTEEN

On a fallen log in the forest, Malaika took a seat and listened as Tomás unraveled a world more complex than she had ever imagined. Beside him, Jiang sat with his arms crossed, a scowl on his face, and an occasional grunt.

"We are two of the members of the Council of Mist Keepers," Tomás said to Malaika.

"Mist Keepers..." Malaika repeated. "So, like...Kifo Kibaya?"

Tomás nodded, "Yes, precisely. There are five of us in total. Well, six... because you are here now."

"So there are others then!?" Malaika nearly jumped from her spot. She wasn't alone! This would be her new family—a family of deities or Mist Keepers.

"You'll meet the others soon, I promise. But we want to make sure you are doing okay as well. We never had a successful Mist Keeper who discovered their talents alone."

"She shouldn't have discovered anything on her own," the giant grumbled next to Tomás.

Tomás hissed, "Well, she did, and now she is here. We must respect that."

"She didn't go through the proper means."

"Because you opted not to train her."

Jiang snarled, "I *had* an apprentice. She is an infiltrator."

"And that apprentice failed. That was your fourth failure, Jiang."

"If you let me do what I wanted, Yūki wouldn't have failed."

"And what about Tovia, Ramiz, and Owen?"

"They all failed after Ningursu's interference," Jiang snarled through his teeth.

"What are you going on about?" Malaika asked. Failure? What did they mean, failure?

"It does not concern you!" Jiang bellowed.

"Jiang is right, Malaika. You do not need to worry about failure, as you are already here as a success story in your own right," Tomás added.

"You need to start talking 'cause I only know names so far."

"Of course, of course." Tomás crossed his legs and leaned forward, peering into the forest as he spoke. "You are already familiar with your talents as a Mist Keeper, so we can avoid that entire lecture. You release souls. It is your duty. And you have performed admirably."

Malaika said nothing, waiting for more.

"Typically, with a new Mist Keeper, they go through an intense training where they learn to wield their power in unique ways...such as your map."

"You know about the map?"

"Our leader, Ningursu, knows all." Tomás paused, picked at his fingernail, then continued. "It's quite impressive, the way you have captured it. Ningursu has been trying to create a map like that for centuries, and he is most excited for you to join our ranks."

Malaika shook her head back and laughed, "Why should I *join* you? I've been fine on my own!"

"Because that's the way it goes," Jiang grumbled from his spot on the log.

"Is killing your potential successor also the way it *goes?*"

"You shouldn't have existed!"

"Jiang, shush!" Tomás snapped, the mist rising around him with a moment of anger. Then, as he recomposed himself, it settled. He turned back to Malaika. "There are only so few Mist Keepers in the world, all of us centuries old. In the grand scheme of life and death, we're each other's constants. There're few others who last for so many centuries."

"I do not know why Ningursu doesn't eliminate them already..." Jiang muttered.

Tomás ignored him, continuing his focus on Malaika. "With so few of us, it is important to stay together. There's only five of us in the Council of Mist Keepers at the moment. We can hardly call ourselves a *council*, to be honest. There's Jiang and me, of course, but also Aelia, Julietta, and Ningursu. We need to stay together to survive because there are forces out there threatening us."

"Like what? A rogue Mist Keeper... like me?" Malaika remained unconvinced. Tomás seemed to beseech her to join. Sure, she loved the idea of being with others, but trust was the product of more than just a smile and a wink. She could not look past what Jiang did—even if it meant she would not be alone.

"No, no, not you. But the world is much more complicated than Life and Death. You must understand that. There are powerful seers, enchanters, and monsters loitering throughout this world that threaten the balance."

"You're speaking in tongues! All of this is the type of thing my father would say to me when trying to get me to marry. 'It's *your* duty, Malaika.' 'Do this for the *betterment* of the family.' 'It's the best option for you.' Blah, blah, blah!" Malaika rose from the log. "Be honest with me. Don't beat around the bush or any of that. Just say point blank that *you* and your posse of Mist Keepers cannot fathom the idea of someone acting independently. Because for however long I've been doing this, I've been absolutely fine. Sure, I get lost daily, but here I am, doing what I need to do."

Tomás didn't speak. Beside him, Jiang smirked. He removed a flask from his hip and took a swift drink, then handed it to Malaika with a grin. She waved it away in disgust.

Malaika ignored the men to summon her map, letting Pam's shadow wrap around her, and searched the area for her next destination. She would probably go back to the town and help souls. That was the best option, right? She could forget this entire interaction and continue her voyage. That was her duty. Not some... *Mist Keeper* responsibility.

Tomás finally spoke, though, "Ningursu requires that you meet with him. I believe it is for your benefit...and it will provide you with the community that you so desire."

"I have my community." Malaika didn't look up from her map, focusing on the area by the docks.

"Do you? I can read your thoughts. I know how alone you've been."

"You can read my thoughts?" Malaika peeked over her map at Tomás.

"Everyone harnesses the mist differently. I read thoughts. Jiang—"

"I do nothing," Jiang snapped.

"Right. Nothing." Tomás continued, "We have some-one who can paint memories in the mist and a healer as well. We're all part of one unit. And we're offering you this community. But...if you do not want that, at least come to meet Ningursu. Are you not at least a bit inter-ested in his tale?"

Malaika frowned, still keeping her attention locked on Tomás. Yes, it would be interesting to learn the true story of Kifo Kibaya. She couldn't deny that learning of this small Council intrigued her, too. After all, she was a part of an exclusive group of individuals. Only five— well, now six—people could claim to be these Mist Keepers? It seemed ridiculous, to be honest.

If anyone had an answer, it would be this leader, Ningursu.

"Very well. I'll speak with him." Malaika said.

"Excellent. We'll leave in the morning. It is a bit of a hike."

Nineteen

Malaika considered fleeing. It'd be so easy to leave behind these ridiculous Mist Keepers. But Tomás had piqued her interest enough to meet with this mysterious Ningursu. After all, now it meant she didn't have to be alone.

So she stayed the night in a small tavern on the coastline, and in the morning, she met with Tomás just outside the building. Jiang did not wait with him, having left to deliver a message to Ningursu about Malaika's arrival. So without arguing, Malaika followed Tomás into the forest and through the mist.

As they traveled, the mist tunneled around them, pushing them across the map. Tomás didn't stop to admire the surrounding world, passing through forests

and towns without blinking. Traveling like this was ex-
hausting, though. While Malaika used the mist to move,
she had spent time resting and observing the world she
traveled through. Her focus had always been on helping
the dead.

But Tomás treated this traveling like a race with a
deadline.

They did not travel in silence. While hopping from
forest to city to river to town, Tomás filled Malaika in on
the history of the Council. He told her how Ningursu
became the first Mist Keeper thousands of years earlier,
and over the years, he built out the mist as a haven for
the dead. In that time, he had accumulated enemies —
immortal enchanters, seers, monsters, and more all
threatened his rule. Before his successor, Aelia, took
over releasing souls, Ningursu had tried to build an army of Mist Keepers. The pressure of the mist caused
most of them to fail.

It made Malaika's success more impressive. With no
proper guidance, she stepped into her role with ease.
Ningursu had spent hundreds of years cumulating his
abilities of all-knowing sight and control of the Mist.
Every Mist Keeper to follow underwent training of their
own as well. When Aelia first joined the mist, she stud-
ied for years with a known alchemist to master her
healing abilities and talents. Tomás then mentioned

that his ability, which allowed him to read and manipulate minds using the mist, nearly caused him to fail his
own apprenticeship. His successor, Julietta, had her
own series of difficulties when she became a Mist Keeper, leading to memory loss and confusion. Jiang too
struggled, although Tomás did not elaborate further on
the giant.

"You adapted well to the mist, and if we can understand why, then future Mist Keepers may have an easier
time adapting. Every loss of an apprentice breaks the
Council further; so many lives have been sacrificed to
the mist...potential lives we never should have lost,"
Tomás said.

"I wish I could tell you why, honestly," Malaika responded.

"There had to be unique circumstances surrounding
your shift into the mist."

"You mean other than that bastard killing me?"

"Yes, besides that." Tomás tiptoed over a log as they
strolled through the forest. Malaika hopped over it behind him, landing firmly on the ground beside him.

"Maybe I'm just that much smarter than all of you,"
Malaika touted.

Tomás shrugged. "Ningursu may know. Or he may
not." He stopped, picking at the bark of the nearby tree.

"Although, sometimes, I cannot help but wonder if the mist is getting smarter."

"What do you mean?"

"It is just a thought...that the mist is perhaps learning from us, and thus allows us to succeed."

"So, the mist is alive now?"

"It has remnants of life throughout it—as both ghosts and others. Such as your dragon friend." Tomás motioned to Pam's shadow flittering behind them.

"You can see Pam!?"

"Sometimes, yes."

Tomás said nothing else. Really, considering how much he spoke, he said little about himself. Malaika learned how he had become a Mist Keeper seven-hundred-fifty years earlier. He detailed his magic, how he could sense thoughts and infiltrate minds. When Malaika inquired about his talent, he waved her fascination away, focusing on telling her about Aelia's ability to understand the human body through the mist.

Malaika hung onto Tomás's every word but moving from town to forest to field to city, anxiety crept over her body. Her map tugged her to different souls, but she had to keep following Tomás, deeper and deeper away from civilization.

The distance grew tighter between her and this so-called Council as they entered the fog-riddled swamp of

Volfium. Tomás moved through the mud like any other surface, almost gliding with the mist on his heels. Malaika stumbled at first but found her footing the further they ventured. She marveled at the trees coated in a vermillion-colored sap while a fog gripped the area with its density. She couldn't move it, not like the mist of the Dead. This mist belonged to the earth and nothing more.

Malaika lost track of how many days they traveled. It blended with each step and story. When alone at night, she would occupy herself with the map, reflecting on Jullian and Tabia. She would get back to Errat someday, that much Malaika had decided. Then she could see their new shop and tell them all about her adventures.

She missed them more than her birth family. At night, she occasionally thought of her mother. But, she was so far removed that their relationship belonged to the stories alone. By now, was Joshi in charge of the farm? Did he have a family? And what of their father—what happened to his trade deal after she left with Pam?

The thoughts left almost as soon as they arrived, and the next morning, her trek through the swamp continued.

After four days, with mud calcified on their shoes, Tomás stopped Malaika outside a thick wall of trees. "We are almost there."

"You said that days ago..." Malaika muttered.

"It takes time to travel through the mist. On foot, this would have taken a month. But now, we are merely one jump to where Ningursu dwells. I do want to prepare you, though."

"Isn't that what you've been doing?"

"Yes, but I want you to be prepared for... horrors."

"Horrors?"

"There are things in this world that lack humanity. Ningursu is a curator of such oddities. So all I ask is that you keep an open mind and wear your bravery with pride."

Malaika scoffed. "If you say so."

Tomás turned back to the wall of trees. Around them, the smoke gathered, pushing forward once again, deeper into the swamp. Malaika stayed close, moving with ease through the trees and letting the mist carry her. It was like riding on the back of the dragon. Pam's shadow rode beside her.

She didn't care what answers lay beyond the veil. She would collect her truths, then move on, back to the existence she had chosen.

The mist parted around them.

Only to be greeted by a graying monster dripping with blood.

TWENTY

The monster opened its mouth and spit a deer skull onto the ground. As the bone fell, a quaking roar escaped the creature's lips. With the scream, the mist turned yellow. Malaika did not step back from it, keeping still as the creature's lopsided yellow eyes darted back and forth, almost glowing on its gray skin. White hair mangled its face while elongated fingernails scratched at the ground. Its breath wreaked of sulfur and rot. Upon noticing Malaika and Tomás, it lurched forward, only to be stopped by a chain around its neck.

Malaika tilted her head to the side. The creature's soul called to her, a mangled conglomerate of different voices begging for her attention. Beneath it all, hiding, was nothing more than a lost child. It was like when she felt Pam's shadow: a distant hum, a soft cry, lost in the woods of their mind.

"Hey there, it's okay. We're just coming to say hello." Malaika said to the monster.

"Leave it alone, Malaika. It's one of Ningursu's monsters." Tomás beckoned her away from it.

Malaika kept her focus on the creature. "Doesn't it have a name?"

"It is nothing more than Diabolo. It does not need a name."

"A what?"

"It is a monster composed of nightmares and terrors. The worst of the worst individuals combined into one body. It is nothing more than that."

"But... I feel a soul in there. Like a child or something!"

"The Diabolo is surely luring you in—it is what it does. There are no children crying for their mothers."

"I never said there were."

Tomás stiffened but didn't reply, instead taking a step down the path away from the monster.

Malaika glanced one last time at this so-called Diabolo. Its eyes remained locked on her. Did it hear her? What was it thinking now? She would have spent more time with it, but Tomás called for her to follow.

"I'll be back later," she whispered to the monster.

If it heard her, it showed no understanding.

The pathway leading deeper into the trees instilled Malaika with greater fear. With every step, her stomach tumbled, and her heart knotted. Sweat gathered on her brow. Every step begged to go backward, leave this swamp, forget about the Mist Keepers. She could create her own kingdom and role. She could create her own world order. Not some... ancient Council.

But with the way the mist beckoned her forward, she knew turning away from it was out of the question. By being here now, she was a member of the Council.

Tomás led her to a clearing where an extensive tree towered above the swamp. Its trunk expanded like the wall of a city, dripping with red sap. At its base, more of the creatures loitered. They did not bear the same anger as the one at the front entrance but rather a distant, glossy stare. Their faces resembled humans, opening and closing their mouths as if mumbling in prayer. Malaika wanted to speak to them, but Tomás tugged her away and around the back of the tree.

Malaika expected the sight behind the tree to enchant her and transport her to one of her mother's stories. She imagined a courtroom, or castle, where Kifo Kibaya loitered.

Instead, only the swamp waited, guarded by none other than Jiang. Two women sat a few paces away on a log, their attention drawn to Tomás and Malaika's arrival.

"Is Ningursu waiting?" Tomás asked.

"He has been for quite a few days," Jiang replied.

"Very good. Come, Malaika."

Yet Malaika didn't follow, glancing at the two women on the log. "Are you gonna introduce me to your colleagues? Aren't they Mist Keepers too?"

"Oh! Right, yes." Tomás paused and motioned to the first woman. With a narrow face and dark hair, her beady eyes bore down at Malaika. "This is Aelia, our healer." He then motioned to the blonde woman beside her, "And this is Julietta, our memory painter."

While the beady-eyed woman did not speak, the blonde woman smiled in Malaika's direction.

"It's a pleasure to meet you, Malaika," Julietta said. "I hope we'll have time to talk soon."

"I look forward to learning more about you," Malaika replied.

The woman's face paled, and her attention dropped to the ground.

Malaika didn't have a chance to say anything else. Tomás beckoned her to follow, so she grumbled to herself, bid goodbye to Aelia and Malaika, then trudged deeper into the swamp beneath the arching trees.

But there still was no grandeur, no pearl flooring, and no castle. Only smoke and mud.

Past the archway, there amid the swamp, stood a ghost.

At first, nothing seemed special about the ghost. Fading in and out, he stood there, his face marred by a thick beard and long hair, without expression.

Then, she noticed the object in his hands: a human head. Skin pulled from the head itself while a single white eye watched Malaika's every movement. Its chapped lips pulled into a smile, extending between its hollow cheeks.

"Ah, Malaika," the skull boomed.

"I imagine you are Ningursu?" Malaika asked.

"Bright, isn't she?" Ningursu smirked at Tomás.

"Yes, she is quite bright indeed."

"Excellent. You are dismissed."

"Yes, sir."

Tomás retreated through the arched trees, leaving Malaika alone with the head.

Ningursu stared at Malaika, long and hard, his gaze like a dagger into her soul. As she stared back at him, a realization struck her. She'd seen this exact head in her map. It was the reason she ventured across the sea in the first place.

"I saw you in my map!" she exclaimed.

"Yes, I sensed you looking at me. I am so glad you have come."

"Why?"

"Why?" Ningursu narrowed his one good eye.

"Yes, why? What does it matter if I am here? I was doing my job, and now I'm not, so souls are suffering."

"Do you not wonder where you come from? What secrets lie in the mist?"

"I've figured it out. There are ghosts, there's mist, and I got to help them out. Not too hard, really. Oh, and you have some nightmarish monsters as well. And sometimes Mist Keepers fail... which is why Jiang went and killed me. Because he already had an apprentice, so he thought I was an imposter."

"You really are quite sharp. All the more reason you should join our council—we need an observant individual like yourself, and with your talent, you would give us all the more strength."

"And why would I do that? You, Tomás, Jiang... all of you have been talking about the Council but have answered nothing yet. Why should I help you? I've been fine on my own." Malaika asked.

Ningursu pondered her question, closing his eye in thought. The silence held the air with the bubbling and croaking of the swamp. The smoke held Malaika in place, and despite her desire to leave, she waited for Ningursu's response.

"I believe you met Julietta when you arrived, yes?" Ningursu finally replied.

"The blonde girl? Yes. She seems nice."

"She was once the most promising Mist Keeper we ever trained. In her apprenticeship, she shimmered like a star or a jewel. But... when the time came, and she entered the mist in full, she lost herself. Ask her any question about her past; she cannot recall it. Her memory only remains for so many years before vanishing." Ningursu simpered, his single eye downcast. "We have lost many Mist Keepers to the overwhelming power of the mist. By joining us, you receive safety and knowledge of everything that may harm you. We vowed, after Julietta's failure, to always help our Mist Keepers."

Malaika narrowed her eyes. "Jiang said his apprentices failed."

"Because he would not let us help."

"No, he said it was after you intervened."

"Oh no, no, he just does not want to admit his own failures."

The answer seemed true enough; Jiang did not hold tight to emotion or empathy, based on Malaika's few interactions with him. But did it align with what she had learned? Could she trust this...head?

"I have not failed yet on my own," Malaika whispered.

"Not yet. But so many of us have succumbed to the mist."

"Have you?"

Ningursu continued, ignoring the question, "You may be fine now, Malaika Jelani... but you will need our support one day. Do not turn away this invitation."

She stared at Ningursu, then at the ghost who carried him. The ghost didn't speak. His dark eyes focused past Malaika and into the trees. His lips remained locked in a permanent frown.

"I don't think I can answer you today," Malaika said.

Ningursu's lip twitched, but he kept his voice level and said, "Return to me in a year. Experience more of this world. Learn more of the Mist Keepers and the dead. Then give me your answer. Is that agreeable?"

Malaika glanced back at the swamp. Pam's shadow wove through the trees, jittery as ever.

"Very well," Malaika said, "I'll return in a year."

TWENTY-ONE

Malaika left the swamp without a word to the other Mist Keepers. They stared after her in silence, as if every one of them already knew what occurred between her and Ningursu. She waved them goodbye, only taking a moment to stop in front of the monster at the front. It stared at her, jaw ajar, yellow eyes bearing into her soul.

"You behave now, y'hear?" she said to it.

The monster snarled.

With that, she bid it goodbye and ventured on with her journey.

And a year passed.

She explored every corner of the Eastern Continent, wrapping around the northern countries of Kainan to Evylain, before venturing back across the sea with Pam's shadow on her heels. She took in every sight, released every good soul, and let her map expand.

Occasionally, when resting for the night, she took a glimpse back at the other Mist Keepers meandering through their secret swamp. She didn't stay long on them. Frankly, they bored her. But she found interest in the monsters chained to the tree, particularly the decrepit one chained to the front entrance of the swampy enclosure. For hours, Malaika found herself transfixed by its yellow eyes and lopsided jaw. Behind its monstrous appearance, a glimmer of humanity lingered. She imagined that the Diabolo once had a family or friends. Was it warm in the swamp? Or in the winter, did it feel cold?

It reminded her of how she perceived Pam as a child. Sure, the dragon scared her at first, but as Malaika observed Pam, she recognized the dragon's true nature. This monster, or Diabolo, as they called it, was the same. Hidden behind a wall of fury, it reacted without a thought. How long had it been a prisoner of the Council?

The more Malaika traveled, the more she thought of the Diabolo. The dragons in Spinoza reminded her of Pam, and her escape with the dragon reminded her of the Diabolo. What were the Mist Keepers hiding about this creature? Were there others like it? As she crossed the smoky plains of Spinoza and through the ice-riddled permafrost of Heims, the idea of the creature became her obsession. She viewed it each night in her map, furiously knitting a scarf to quell her nerves.

To be honest, when she first left the swamp, she had no intentions of ever returning. The idea of joining the Council held no appeal. But with the Diabolo weaving its way through her thoughts over the growing months, she turned south again towards Volfium to let her map guide her back into the swamp.

She would have arrived sooner if the Newbird mountains in Rosada did not distract her with their thick smoke and graying trees.

But she still returned to the Council.
Even though a year had passed, nothing changed. The swamp greeted her with the same bloody scowl, and at the front of the enclosure, the Diabolo waited, reeling against its chains and the tree.

"Hullo again." Malaika held her hands out as she approached it. Pam's shadow quivered between the trees.

The Diabolo shrieked, stretching its neck against the chains.

"I'm not gonna hurt you or nothing. I promise. Just want to make sure you're okay. If that's all good by you, that is."

Another shriek followed.

"Listen, I know you're scared. I'm...I'm gonna figure out what to do about this. I promise."

The Diabolo showed no sign of understanding, continuing to struggle against its chains. One eye remained locked on Malaika.

Malaika kept her hands out. "I know you got no reason to trust me. But... I'm a friend. I promise."

The Diabolo continued its obnoxious cries.

She took a step forward, extending her hand to the monster.

It paused, transfixed on her fingers.

"Malaika! What do you think you're doing?"

She turned. Aelia stood between the trees, a collection of jars and vials on her belt, filled with silver and gold.

"Just talking to the Diabolo," Malaika stepped away from the monster and turned to Aelia. "There's a human under there."

"Not anymore. Do not occupy yourself with such silly endeavors."

"Have you ever tried?!"

"Of course I have tried. I have been working with Teodozia here for hundreds of years." Aelia's gaze did not waver, hard and focused.

"Teodozia?"

"That's her name."

"She has a name?"

"Of course she has a name. She was a Mist Keeper."

Twenty-Two

Aelia led Malaika back to Ningursu. Despite Malaika's probes about Teodozia, Aelia did not reply, repeating the same message: "Ningursu will tell you what is necessary."

Malaika huffed with frustration but kept her complaints to herself, bringing her attention once again to the head sitting on a stump in the middle of the murky waters. His ghostly companion stood beside him, hands laced behind his back, expression blank.

After Aelia left, Ningursu spoke, "Welcome back, Malaika."

She didn't reply.

"Have you made your decision?"

Malaika glanced over her shoulder, trying to catch a glimpse of Teodozia or any of the monsters, but the mist proved too thick. "You mentioned the failures of Mist Keepers last time I was here. But you did not mention Teodozia."

"Oh yes, the Diabolo."

"If I do not join you, will I become like Teodozia?" Malaika turned back to Ningursu, observing him. "Is that what you meant by *failure?*"

Ningursu stared past Malaika, deep into the swamp, opening and closing his mouth as he searched for a response. His next statement came calculated, almost rehearsed in its delivery, as if said countless times. "Teodozia is a unique situation. She was quite a young girl at the time. At that age, she easily succumbed to her nightmares and became what you see now. While others have failed, they have not all followed the same path as Teodozia."

"And you don't think I'll become the same as Teodozia?"

"As long as you trust us, you will not. We have safeguards in place to prevent such... anomalies from occurring again."

"Like what?"

"Our members, of course. Jiang has muscle, Julietta can harness memories, Tomás can enter your mind, Aelia can brew cures, and I understand the mist to its core. We can offer you that protection, Malaika. That is what I meant a year ago, and it is what I promise you now." Ningursu blinked once. Around him, smoke gathered for a second, like a set of arms welcoming Malaika into an embrace. "By joining us, you get that protection."

Malaika took a small step away from him. "What if I don't need your protection?"

The black smoke fell.

Malaika continued, "I had no intentions of returning here, to be honest. Your council has no appeal to me. I'm not encountering anything that causes me duress or any difficulties with being a Mist Keeper. Really, I've been doing great. But..." Malaika fidgeted with the cuff of her shirt. She needed to find the word that would satisfy Ningursu as he sat there, black smoke fizzling in and out from his orifices. She didn't want to know what he could do with the Mist. How would he react to the true reason she wanted to return? Her interest sat solely around Teodozia. Like Pam, the Diabolo had no means of escape. But, like Pam, Teodozia had Malaika now. "But knowing what could become of me has created a newfound fear. I would hate to be a... monster."

Ningursu's lip twitched. "So, you shall join us?"

"I will be available to you," Malaika recited. "My job requires me to travel the world, doesn't it? So I'll commit to visiting once per year. After all... what is a year in the life of a god?"

Ningursu accepted Malaika's offer after an hour of trying to convince her to visit more than once a year. Once he finally settled, he asked to see her map, which she showed with hesitancy. He observed every corner, not speaking, as she enhanced the image of different parts of the world.

"I am glad you have agreed to this arrangement," he finally remarked.

And with that, he bid her goodbye.

Malaika trudged from the swamp enclosure without a word. Even as she passed Aelia, Tomás, and Jiang, she didn't stop to speak with or acknowledge them. They would see her plenty, but right now, she wanted to see only one other.

Teodozia had not left her spot. Not that Malaika expected her to leave, but there was a momentary hope that the Diabolo had escaped. But the chains remained stable, and as Malaika approached her, she noticed the strange smoke-like quality of the restraints, like the smoke Ningursu had produced earlier.

The Diabolo shrieked again at Malaika's presence.

"I know you don't trust me, but I promise I'm a good one, alright? I'm gonna find a way to help you."

Another bellow.

If only she could show the Diabolo that she understood, that the nightmares might be heavy and painful, but that they did not define her.

But those terrors had overwhelmed the person inside Teodozia's body.

"Look, here, this will help when it gets cold. Don't know if it gets cold often here, but I'm sure there's a freeze occasionally. Here..." Malaika reached into her bag and removed a knit shawl. Willing her hands to remain calm, she handed the shawl to Teodozia.

The Diabolo yanked the shawl from Malaika. Her fingernails caught the lace, ready to tear the yarn to pieces.

But as Teodozia's fingers grazed the soft texture, she stopped and carefully brought the shawl to her cheek.

"Mmm!" Teodozia exclaimed.

Malaika grinned, "It's comfy, right? I always think so."

"Mmm! Mmmmm."

"You can keep it. I'll bring you another next time, alright?"

Teodozia continued to fawn over the shawl, seeming to forget that Malaika stood there.

Malaika patted the Diabolo's cold, gray hand. A spark of life pinched at her fingertips.

There, deep within the surface of Teodozia's soul, a child laughed.

TWENTY-THREE

Wandering became her signature.

Malaika traveled across the world, mapping the mist with Pam's shadow on her heels. Pam served as her companion, constantly on her side as she traveled up and down the continents, visiting foreign cities and meeting unfamiliar faces. She relished each new location: from crystalized city to towering glasses of sand, to plains filled with mist and smoke. Pam never left her side. Although just a shadow of her former glory, the dragon gave Malaika the solace of a constant friend. Pam would never leave her side.

Yet, Malaika often wondered at night, while observing parts of her map, if the dragon was happy. Pam would fly away each morning, and when Malaika checked her map, the dragon ventured far and wide, skimming the ground as if searching for something. Despite her flight, she always returned to Malaika at sunset. *If only I could understand you, Pam, then I might be able to help.*

She never told Pam to stay, but the dragon followed her day after day, month after month, and year after year. Occasionally she flew off, and Malaika swore it would be the last time she saw the dragon, but Pam always returned. She never found what she was looking for, instead returning to what was familiar.

How can I help her? Malaika often wondered as Pam flew into the sky. She couldn't be sure what lingered in Pam's heart. *You're free, Pam. You do not have to stay by my side if you do not want to stay.*

The only time the dragon shied away was when Malaika visited the Council of Mist Keepers in Volfium, as she promised Ningursu. Even when Malaika didn't want to return, an invisible gnawing drew her back to the Council. Part of it was her longing to see Teodozia, but something else also tugged at her soul. It was as though someone had tethered her to the Council, trapping her in the repetitive motion of visiting.

She sat with Teodozia every time she visited. During the first few years, the monster showed no signs of remembering her. Yet, Malaika continued to leave behind knitted items for the winter, and the Diabolo picked them up with excitement.

By the fifth year, Teodozia came to expect the gift, and when Malaika handed her a knit hat, she grabbed it with an excited shriek. She placed it on her head, squishing her stringy white hair underneath its brim, before smiling at Malaika with hole-filled teeth.

Other than Teodozia, Malaika spoke little to the other Mist Keepers. Occasionally Tomás would make small talk, and of course Ningursu would probe her with each visitation, but otherwise, they were strangers. Aelia showed no interest. If present, Aelia spent most of her time collecting the strange red sap on the trees or filling vials with swamp water. Malaika could only assume it had to do with her healing magic… or something along those lines.

Jiang rarely showed his face. Meanwhile, Julietta would walk in a haze through the swamp, smiling at Malaika with no real acknowledgment. It was a strange council indeed. Wouldn't it make more sense if they all spent their time releasing souls from terror? Perhaps they did, sometimes at least. But Malaika had checked her map enough to know how stationary they all remained. Not including Jiang, they never moved farther than a day's distance from the swamp.

She didn't keep track of the years. It didn't matter, really. In death, time meant nothing. When the world could shift beneath her with a single flick of her finger, seasons had no rhythm. Location had no sense.

She was Kifo Kibaya, riding the back of eternal youth, masked by a mist of death. What did it matter what year it was... especially when all her friends were dead, too?

So Malaika couldn't be sure how many years had passed when she delivered Teodozia a sweater. Upon handing it to her, Teodozia stared at the item before placing it on her head.

"No, not like that!" Malaika laughed. She approached Teodozia and held out her hands. "Here, let me help."

For the first time, Teodozia bowed her head, allowing Malaika to help the sweater over her skin. She held her breath as a plume of yellow smoke escaped the Diabolo's lips, catching her hair in a gasp. When the Diabolo's breath caught her, it was like being pulled back into her nightmares; she was disoriented and misplaced, wandering alone.

But then it passed, and she stood there with Teodozia, adjusting the sweater.

"There you go," Malaika stepped back from the Diabolo. "Nice and warm now, right?"

Teodozia hugged herself, taking in the woolen exterior of the sweater.

"See, I'm gonna help you. I'm your friend."

Teodozia remained too enthralled with her sweater to respond.

Malaika sank back onto a log, watching the Diabolo. She really was like a child, brimming with interest and fascination. Nightmares gathered on her skin, but they did not define her; a mere product of misfortune, she wore these nightmares like a permanent scar. The Council judged her. But for what? A mistake? A failure? Ningursu spoke of supporting Malaika if she failed. Is this what it would look like—a Diabolo?

"Ah, I never seen Teodozia look so happy," a soft voice said.

Malaika turned. Julietta stood there, a canvas under her arm and a paintbrush behind her ear. A haunting emptiness glossed over her green eyes.

"Oh, Julietta, hullo." Malaika stepped away from Teodozia.

Julietta approached Teodozia, undeterred by her monstrous nature. She removed her paintbrush and stroked it through the air, gathering mist on it like paint. Humming to herself, she painted a scene in the air of a child standing at the edge of a beach, laughing while yellow smoke surrounded her.

Seconds later, the painting vanished.

"What was that?" Malaika asked.

"The last time she was happy, of course. When she was becoming a Mist Keeper and learning to harness the mist. She didn't know it would be her last time... happy..." Julietta blinked a few times. "She thought she understood it... but oh, she was wrong."

"But she's happy now." Malaika glanced up at Teodozia, still hugging the sweater close.

"She is happy now. It's a shame that Aelia couldn't keep her happy."

"What?"

"Aelia was her predecessor. Teodozia thought Aelia would care for her forever... but... it was all a lie. A brilliant, horrible lie." Julietta placed her canvas against a nearby tree. "What a shame... what a shame..."

"What do you mean a lie?" Malaika kept pressing.

"It was before me. The lie, that is. And Teodozia's memory is jumbled. But... I believe that power, selfishness, and fear cause people to behave in unfavorable ways. Such terrible ways..." Julietta sighed before continuing. "Teodozia did not fit the mold. So Aelia and Ningursu had to reshape her."

"And turn her into this?"

"If memory serves correct, then yes... yes indeed." Julietta stared at Malaika. For the first time, it really felt like the woman *saw* Malaika. She always appeared aloof,

136

but here and now, Julietta was present. "Be wary of your differences. Ningursu will make you comply."

"Wait... what do you mean? Am I at risk of becoming like Teodozia?"

Julietta did not reply, her face falling back into a haze as she removed a jar of paint from her apron and began to detail a swamp on her blank canvas.

TWENTY-FOUR

Panic swept over Malaika, and with her heart racing, she bounded from the swamp and into the mist. She moved in a haze, releasing souls, and hopping between towns, all while her mind continued to circle in fear over the following days. What did Julietta mean by "be wary"? Would Ningursu really turn Malaika into something like Teodozia? Lost... confused... and empty?

Sleep battled with fear, leaving her awake well into the night. It might be unfounded, she knew that much, but she couldn't shake the panic in her chest. Only when Pam's shadow lay beside her, a constant in her life, did she finally sink into the peace of sleep. Ningursu could not follow her. He was a skull! He never left his spot in the swamp. As long as she did her job, then certainly he wouldn't come after her.

And what could he do anyway? She had seen his black smoke exploding from his mouth and the chains that kept Teodozia locked in place. But really, she had seen little of his talents in action. It might all be a ploy to scare her.

No, she just had to keep doing her job and reporting to him once per year. Then she would be safe.

And even if he grew displeased with her, she had the map. If he sent anyone after her, she would see them coming for her. Although Ningursu never appeared on it, everyone else did. She had the means to escape.

I'm safe. I have done nothing wrong. Do not let Julietta ignite you with fear. She closed her eyes, resting in a tavern for the night. Already, she had been skeptical of Ningursu. This would only do well to place her on high alert.

While in the stories her mother told her, Kifo Kibaya always tried to help, they were only stories. They never described Kifo Kabaya as a talking skull. Yes, they called him a faceless shadow, shifting in and out of the mist, perhaps. But not a bodiless head.

Was he an imposter? Did the real Kifo Kibaya wait in the mist?

And if so... then where was Uzyma? Would she rise one day to balance life and death?

I can't let Ningursu dictate my future. I can decide my purpose. Malaika shut her eyes tight. She'd come this far on her own. There was no reason to turn her back on her choices now.

If Ningursu didn't like them, well, she wasn't afraid of some bodiless head.

The world became her fortress. As the years passed, Malaika learned of the best chocolate, the warmest coffee, and the smoothest wine. She reserved rooms in her favorite taverns, all while visiting the friends—both alive and dead—she made along the way.

But, of all the places, she still loved returning to Errat to visit Jullian and Tabia.

Over the years, they had grown their little general store, where the dead would visit to collect goods. Malaika didn't quite know what ghosts needed to exist—perhaps a taste of food or a change of clothes every now and again. That was a world she had never understood: the life of the truly dead.

She asked Tabia once how it felt, but the woman merely replied, "Oh, it feels like the wind."

Malaika didn't even try to understand. So she accepted the answer with a mere nod.

Jullian and Tabia showed no distaste for Malaika's state of existence. In some ways, they seemed sorry for her. Whenever she returned to Errat, Jullian once remarked about the weight on Malaika's shoulders, with a hope that someday she might find the freedom of peace.

Only now, with the truth about Teodozia heavy in her heart, did Malaika understand what Jullian meant.

A few moons after learning the truth from Julietta, she arrived in Errat. Upon entering the gates of the city, Pam's shadow took to the side, signaling her arrival to those who cared. Malaika never wrote to announce her arrival; she never timed it properly, getting lost on the way to Errat in more instances than not.

But with Pam in the sky, Jullian and Tabia had learned of Malaika's arrival.

This time, they did not wait for her on the front step of the general store, leaving Malaika to enter without knocking. Above her head, the bell rang.

"Hullo?" she called into the shop, "Jullian? Tabia? It's me."

She checked behind the counter and between the shelves. *No one.*

"Hullo!?" she called again as she climbed up the stairs. The hollow beats of emptiness echoed around her, dust gathering in the air.

Malaika peeked into each room. Emptiness greeted her.

When she entered her old bedroom, she found a single piece of paper on the blanket, with Tabia's writing scribbled across it.

Our dearest Malaika,

The time came sooner than we expected to move into the gods' embrace. Even death can be tiring, and we have done our good duty over these last few decades. The shop will be our legacy. Already, we have sent letters to some of our dear friends, asking that they keep the shop running in our stead.

We had hoped to see you one last time before fading, but the circumstances would not allow it. As we secured our legacy, our will to stay full vanished with the mist.

Our paths have diverged. Your life has taken you on a weaving journey, one that does not allow you to be a permanent fixture in the lives of many. Jullian saw it when he first met you. Like the dragon you freed, your destiny commands that you take flight.

But heed these words, Malaika. You cannot save everyone. We know how much you want to help the monster you spoke to us about, but if it is not in your fate, then do not pursue it.

Yet, these words will not stop you. Rather, you will continue to soar.

So while we are gone, please remember how proud we are of you. We are glad that we helped free you and helped to guide you into this new role.

We are sure your parents would be proud.

And we love you dearly, Malaika.

So be safe.

Be good.

And be free.

We'll watch you from forever,
Jullian and Tabia

Malaika stared at the words. A single tear fell from her eye, landing on the page, smudging the ink. She wiped her eyes at once, then rolled the letter like a map and placed it in her bag.

Twenty-Five

Without Jullian and Tabia, Errat no longer felt like home. Malaika completed her duties, releasing the dead into the mist, then left the city almost as fast as she arrived. Her thoughts hung empty in the air, meaningless as she wandered across the plains and into the northern desert. One of the constant things in her life had vanished without a chance to say goodbye.

Only Pam's shadow remained, nestling by her side at night, puffs of smoke expanding from her nostrils. Pam offered no solutions, though; more than anything, Malaika wanted to talk to Jullian and Tabia about Teodozia. Now, she had nothing but her own precognition.

This loss felt different from the first time Jullian and Tabia passed. It was almost like she knew they would wait for her in the afterlife. But now, they had returned to where they belonged, into the arms of Uzyma, Asani Azzan, Nea Reth, Ambar, and Kifo Kibaya. At last, part of the earth again, they could rest in prosperity.

But if the Council of Mist Keepers proved anything, it was that Malaika would never get that type of rest. She would be stuck, forever a servant to the dead, even if not tethered to a council in a swamp.

All she could do was wander, release souls, and continue composing her map, holding Jullian and Tabia's last words close to her heart.

We are sure your parents would be proud. The sentence stuck to Malaika's mind like glue. Would they be proud? She had stolen their dragon, left home without a thought, and never returned. Even through all her voyages, she never stepped foot on that farm again.

Yet now, her parents haunted her waking thoughts. Jullian and Tabia mentioned in their letter how decades had passed since death. Had it really been that long? Time had become such a foreign entity to Malaika. Were her parents even alive anymore? What about Joshi? Why hadn't she taken a moment to think about them in all these years?

She'd been so focused on the souls, on Pam, and on Teodozia that she had forgotten about her first home.

So, from Errat, with a heavy heart, she headed north, back to Leega and to her hometown of Emrys. The roads still held a familiarity. Even with new buildings and fresh flowers, she remembered each path.

Although, she still couldn't recall exactly where each one led. She'd gotten lost on these roads plenty, coming home late in the day to her mother's sighs and father's shouts. While she could pull her map out now, she chose to get lost in the streets, releasing souls of familiar faces—the old shopkeeper, the butcher, and the cobbler, to name a few—and setting them free into the mist.

Her joints quaked at the idea of returning to the farm. Every step dragged like weights, and her heart pounded with daggers. Pam's shadow watched from the sky, like a storm cloud following her every movement.

She didn't take the main road to the farm, instead ducking into the tree line as she walked. The forest still held a familiar essence, bustling with cedar and pine. She wove between the trees, stroking the bark as she walked. As a child, she used to pretend to play games with Uzyma. Now, she walked among them as Kifo Kibaya.

As she strode through the forest, she stumbled over a few murky jars on the ground. A smile inched over her lips as she knelt beside them, gathering one in her hands. Filled with faded dye, she remembered these jars well. Her mother asked her to retrieve them from town, and then she learned of her father's trade. She might have misinterpreted it at the time, but without the trade, she might have never ended up where she stood now.

She dumped the foul liquid from the jar and placed it into her bag before continuing along toward the farm. Part of her wanted to go cover herself in mud, disguise herself as Uzyma all over again, just as she had all those years ago. But she couldn't pretend to be Uzyma anymore.

She wasn't a child.

Instead, she walked in stride, emerging from the forest to a browning field. The baobab trees sat dead on the edge of the farm, and except for a barn filled with a couple of cows, no other animals loitered on the field. If she hadn't known any better, she wouldn't have recognized the farm at all.

But the farmhouse still looked the same, and with the mist as her disguise, she approached it without fear. The door opened.

It was like stepping into the past. The house still had the same furniture, with only a new furnace to signify any passing of time. Against the wall, the fireplace burned with tepid flames, casting a glow throughout the parlor and towards the stairwell. As Malaika entered, the floorboards creaked.

"Hullo?" she called out, letting the mist drop around her. "Is anyone home?"

She half expected the same outcome as in Errat; an empty home, a vacant letter, and another wallop of loneliness.

But this time, a shadow rose from a chair.

The voice of an old man croaked from the darkness, "Who's there?"

Malaika moved into the light to get a look at who spoke. "Joshi?"

An old man stood there with gray hair, a wrinkled face, and an arched back. But his eyes were still the same; the harsh, beady eyes of her brother bore into her soul.

"Malaika? Is that you?" he whispered.

"Yes. Hullo, Joshi."

She expected him to curse at her, to rant and rave.

But the old man approached her.

Only for an embrace.

TWENTY-SIX

A fter you left," Joshi said as he lit a candle, "things changed. Papa searched all over the country for you, forgetting about that trade. Mama...well, she saw you leave but didn't know where you went either. We missed you, Malaika, really."

"I thought you would be mad at me," Malaika whispered.

"We were. Father planned to send you off the moment he found you, but as time passed... I guess he just wanted to know you were safe." Joshi sat down with a grunt. "He died about five years after you left."

I was already...this...when he died...and I don't remember releasing his soul, Malaika thought but didn't say out loud.

Joshi continued, "I took over the farm, got married, had some kids. Mama was around for a few more years before falling ill. At least we were a bit of a family, but Mama always waited to see if you'd return. Her illness took her fast, and I was left with the farm here and my kids and wife. You would've liked my wife; Dalila was her name. Same spunky attitude. Guess I needed a bit of resistance in my life." Joshi chuckled. "She died a few years ago, and my kids all left on their own adventures. Didn't want to tie them down to this failing farm."

"The farm is failing?" Malaika asked.

"Hard to get another dragon after you took Pam away. Spinozan traders don't really trust us. All the more reason for Papa to be mad at you, but... family's more important in the end." Joshi shook his head. "What happened to you, Malaika? You don't look much older than when you left. Am I just finally succumbing to my age here?"

Malaika placed a hand on her brother's arm. A spark passed through her fingers. *Soon.*

"Would you believe me if I told you I am Kifo Kibaya?" she asked him.

"So I guess I am succumbing to it," Joshi sighed. "Serves me right. Haven't talked to my kids since they left. Didn't even bother to write. Just been sitting here, waiting for my death. If I hadn't been such a prick to you, then you wouldn't have left, right? Then Papa would've died happy, and Mama would've been smiling, and this farm wouldn't be so dead."

"Don't blame yourself," Malaika muttered. "You might have been a prick, but we were kids."

"I was eighteen. An adult. But I behaved like a child."

"Not that I was any wiser."

Joshi smirked and closed his eyes. It was strange, seeing him like this; Malaika still pictured her brother as young and smug with not a regret in the world. But time had passed. He had grown older, and she had grown wiser. They could do nothing more but accept the fates laid before them.

"I've wondered in my age if we would have become friends in the end."

"Depends if Papa shipped me far away."

"Oh, you would have crawled back here."

"Or maybe I would have ended up in the same place."

"As Kifo Kibaya?" Joshi laughed. "Ridiculous idea. You just look like my sister."

"And what should Kifo Kibaya look like?"

"Towering and powerful." Joshi chuckled. "I should be quaking in my boots, not thinking myself bonkers."

"It'd be hard to be Kifo Kibaya if I were a giant. Too easy to trample over people. My height lets me sneak in and out unseen."

"You always were a little sneak. Stealing things from my room, spying on the farm, stealing the dragon... sneaky little girl..." he chuckled again, still not opening his eyes. "I suppose death needs to sneak around a bit. Catch you by surprise."

"But this time, I'm not sneaking..." Malaika gulped, holding back a few tears. "I'm here to guide you, Joshi. The moments are thinning."

"Well, that's not much of a surprise. Knew it would come soon. Then the government will claim this land and do what it may with it. Not that it's worth much of nothing at this point." Joshi continued to smile. "I hope Kifo Kibaya will be kind to me."

Malaika sniffled. "Yes, Kifo Kibaya will be kind to you. You've paid your dues."

Joshi's smile did not shift, and with heavy woven breaths, he let silence become his final word. Malaika sat beside him, listening as his breath slowed to sleep before hiccoughing to a halt. Death did indeed arrive in peace, and with Malaika at his side, Joshi passed with ease.

Years ago, Malaika might have left her brother in his horrifying dreams. Now, she had no reservations. With a careful hand, she offered a hand through the maze of Joshi's mind, leading him out of darkness and back towards the mist and light.

It was like any other release, but this one, she did not rush. She let her brother come to terms with his death, face his horrors, and escape the maze with a gentle hand.

Once Joshi escaped his horrors and stood in the mist, Malaika stepped to the side. Around them, the mist thickened. Other figures emerged from the mist. An unfamiliar woman—whom Malaika could only assume was Dalila—as well as her parents waited for Joshi on the other side.

"Mama? Papa?" She squinted at them through the mist.

They grinned at her.

"But how? I never released your souls!"

"Kifo Kibaya came to us. Strong, mighty, and tall," her father whispered.

"He welcomed us here as you helped Joshi," her mother added. "Thank you for coming back to us, Malaika."

"Jiang?" Malaika mumbled. *Is Jiang still releasing souls? Does he not trust me?* As much as she wanted to be angry with him, she couldn't help but thank the giant. If he hadn't released her mother and father, they might still have been rotting in their nightmares.

"What was that, dear?" her mother asked.

"Nothing. It's...lovely to see you again." Malaika squeezed her mother's hand.

"It is indeed...but it is time for us to go." Her mother released Malaika's hand and nodded to Joshi. "Come, we've been waiting."

"But—"

Her mother and father smiled at her before turning back to the mist. Joshi reached for the unfamiliar woman's hand, thanked Malaika with a bow of his head, then disappeared after them.

The mist fell.

Only to leave Malaika alone with Joshi's dead body in an empty house.

TWENTY-SEVEN

Pam's shadow waited for Malaika at the edge of the farmland. Upon seeing the dragon, Malaika knelt beside her, pressing her nose against her smoky skin.

"They're all leaving, Pam. Every one of them... they're gone. I've only got the Council, but... they're just... there." She wiped her eyes and glanced up at the dragon. "Was this what Ningursu meant when he said I would need them?"

The dragon huffed, nudging Malaika with the tip of her snout.

There, Malaika stayed until the morning, sleeping against Pam's shadow, using the weight of the last few months as a blanket. Even in death, her friendships would be temporary. No one lasted forever; their souls yearned for peace, and on their own accord, they decided when to leave.

What if she could have a say when the next person left? In the morning, as she rested beside the dragon, her mind raced. Pam had been loyal to her all these years, but she knew the dragon wanted more. She saw the way Pam took flight and searched the skies. Did she yearn for the same peace as Jullian, Tabia, and Joshi?

Malaika couldn't speak dragon, so how would she know?

But perhaps she could give Pam the choice...on her own terms.

Malaika summoned her map. North of Leega waited Spinoza, marred by fire and dragons. She had passed through it before, releasing souls and staying in different towns, like anywhere else on the globe. There, she would admire the carved cliffs and dancing dragons before venturing further along the continent, continuing her duties.

It only made sense to head north toward Spinoza again.

After all, she had a duty to attend.

The trip to Spinoza proved uneventful, as usual. Malaika moved from town to town like any other day. She would stop by the taverns and shops she'd grown familiar with, taking silent note of the aging shopkeepers and bartenders. The world moved on without her, and she was stuck in a permanent state of existence. No matter who she met, it came with the ongoing promise: someday, they would leave.

So, upon arriving in a little town carved from the corpse of a dragon, she expected the worst.

Pam's shadow flew over her before perching on the tremendous skull marking the entrance to town. Malaika reached for Pam's nose and stroked it, her attention fixated on the smoke-riddled plains north of the town. There, shadows of dragons moved against the graying landscape, capturing the bone-like trees in gasps of smoke. Sometimes, out of the haze, a living dragon would race to the sky, casting the clouds ablaze with the glow of fury.

Unlike when Malaika grew up, these dragons wore their freedom. She'd seen them in her travels already, but now, sitting here with Pam, she could take a moment to revel in their beauty. This is the life Pam should have lived all those years ago, not coped up on a farm, her wings tied together, forced to eat skewered meat. No, she should have been here. Free. With her friends and family.

Sitting outside of town, Malaika turned to Pam.

"If you want to go, then go. You've stayed by my side for so many years... but you deserve your peace too." Malaika smiled at the dragon, "Really, it's okay if you leave. I'll be okay."

Pam tilted her shadowy head to the side. She leaned forward to press her nose against Malaika's cheek. '

"You've been a good girl, Pam. Really. But... I know you want more. 'Cause you're like me. You want adventure, but you also want safety and friendship and..." Malaika inhaled, stopping the tears from falling. "But y'know, promise me you'll say hello when I come on by every now and again. This isn't goodbye. It's a... see you around, alright? Because... this is what you want, and I don't want to hold you back. Okay? Fly. Be more than my shadow. Be you."

The dragon stared off into the smoke, watching the other shadows in awe. No one moved. Not a sound followed.

Until a dragon in the distance screeched.

Pam responded with the same enthusiasm.

"Go," Malaika said, "Please."

Pam nuzzled Malaika once more, then rose onto her feet. The air hung still, and all waited in a pause. Malaika did not breathe.

With a single roar, Pam lifted into the air. Her wings flapped once, and with a gust of mist, she vanished into the dragon-filled plains of Spinoza.

Twenty-Eight

Malaika didn't stay in Spinoza. Really, she didn't stay anywhere, constantly moving across the map, releasing souls, and vowing to negate any commitments. The people she met became ghosts, and only the Council remained as the single constant in her life. They always remained steady in that swamp, waiting for her over each passing year. She had no desire to return to them, but the fact remained: they were there when no one else existed.

At least then, when she visited, she could spend time with Teodozia. The monster remained the same, her smoky chains lassoing her to the ground, preventing any breath of freedom. After meeting with Ningursu, Malaika would sit with Teodozia for hours. She couldn't figure out how to free the monster from the chains.

There was no lock, no key; the chains themselves behaved like appendages extending from Teodozia's body.

Instead, she told stories to the monster, yearning that one day she might reclaim her humanity and speak. At times, Teodozia mouthed along with Malaika, testing the different sounds in her vocal chords.

Yet even that effort proved fruitless, derailed by Aelia one day.

"It's not worth your time, Malaika," Aelia said.

"She can talk—I know it!"

"No. She can't. She is nothing more than a confused personification of nightmares."

Malaika grumbled. When she returned a year later, any progress she had made disappeared. Nothing really changed. Like on her map, borders shifted, but the land always remained constant.

And as years transgressed, the world became less fascinating. Malaika knew the corners of each continent, the way the mountains crawled to the sky, and the weaving emptiness of the canyons. Only Uzyma cast change; wars came, children grew, and flowers died. Life continued.

On...

And on...

Malaika accepted it, hiding in the mist even as she arrived in an empty field marred by war. Black and white flowers scoured the area, dripping with blood from the ensnaring battles. She walked among them, letting her map guide her to souls begging for a release. Even after all these years, releasing souls gave her that flicker of happiness. At least she still held onto the tale; she was Kifo Kibaya, and she would carry that story forever.

Her map guided her to the body of a soldier lying in the field. Beside the body, another soldier leaned over to say his goodbyes. It didn't faze her in the slightest; she'd walked undetected into funerals and memorials. The mist protected her unless she wanted to be seen.

So she strode forward with no real worry. The soldier remained hunched over the body and did not move, tears falling into his thick beard. His fingers rested on his comrade's temples.

"It's okay...it's okay. I'm here," the soldier whispered.

Malaika joined the soldier's side, readying her hand by the dead body. But before she could venture into his terrors, the mist rose around them.

Like a gasp, it parted, revealing the dead soldier's ghost hovering in the air. The ghost reached for the living soldier, placed a hand on his shoulder with a smile, then disappeared back into Uzyma's arms.

"Goodbye, my friend," the soldier whispered, dropping the body to the ground. He blinked the tears away from his face, smiled to himself, then turned in Malaika's direction.

He jumped to his feet. "Who are you!? When did you get here!?"

Malaika climbed to her feet. "I think I have the same question for you."

"What? I was here for hours!"

"Yes, but how long have you been able to release the dead?"

"You mean...you saw that?"

"Of course I saw it—that's my job!"

"Your job? Since when?"

"Since a hundred years ago or something like that. I don't keep track of time."

The soldier didn't move from his spot. "Who are you?"

She grinned, "My name is Malaika Jelani. I am a Mist Keeper...and I think this means...you are like me as well."

The man introduced himself to her as Szyman Gutnik. A tall, burly man with a curly blond beard and messy hair, he was the exact opposite of the well-composed members of the Council. Really, it gave Malaika all the more reason to like him. As they strode back to his campsite, he waved his hands as he spoke, unraveling to Malaika with unbridled excitement.

"I've always had magic. I can create 'replicas' of towns and move them. I always mocked it up to some illusionist ability or something." He said as they arrived at the campsite. With everyone else asleep, and a fire dwindling, they spoke in a hushed voice amid the war-torn plains. He continued, with his gaze fixated on the flame. "A few weeks ago, we were ambushed by a group of Kainan soldiers. Four of our people were killed, and when we were burying them... I suddenly sensed their soul. Does that make any sense to you?"

"It makes perfect sense. It kinda pulled you forward, right? As if helping someone who is lost?"

"Yes, I felt it pulling toward me, but...it was more like someone looking for shelter, and I helped them build a new house."

"Same thing, different feeling." Malaika eyed Szyman. It was strange, seeing another Mist Keeper not embedded in the Council. Did Ningursu know about him? Was it even time for another Mist Keeper to take her place? All the others had hundreds of years between them, but Szyman was only one hundred years her junior.

Malaika continued, "I am excited to have a friend in all of this. Tomorrow, when the sun rises, I can show you more of the mist if you want. You have a world at your disposal now."

Szyman's expression didn't change. "Do I want the world at my disposal?"

"Why wouldn't you?"

"It seems like a burden."

Malaika swallowed. It was a burden. That much was true.

Would she dare force this life on anyone else?

"Well, I won't force you to do anything you don't want, but at least let me tell you about what is waiting in the mist. That way, you are best equipped to handle whatever may come your way. Because I know more than anyone that this mist can take you by surprise. Like you've taken me by surprise. Your magic... I would love to see it!"

Szyman rubbed his beard, nodding to himself. "Very well. In the morning. I need time to rest."

TWENTY-NINE

Once the sun rose, Malaika and Szyman ventured back onto the black-and-white checkered field known as the Schanifeld. There, the mist gathered, dancing through the air and encompassing both the Mist Keepers. As they walked, Malaika told Szyman about the Council and the years she had spent wandering. She tried to contain her excitement: finally, a Mist Keeper not indoctrinated by Ningursu and the Council. Someone like her, someone in whom she could confide.

Szyman listened, hands laced behind his back as he walked beside her. When she finished talking, a smile spread over his face. "Sounds like this council is filled with obstinate fools."

"They're old and stuck in the past."

"Aren't you?"

"Rude! I'm not that old!"

"You said you've been doing this about one hundred years."

"Yes, but the next youngest is four hundred years older than me."

"Four hundred years?" Szyman furrowed his brow. "Are all of them that far apart in age?"

"I think so... why?"

"Well, isn't it peculiar that we are so close in age? What does that mean?"

Malaika frowned. "I... don't know. I may have to ask Ningursu."

"Ah, I see." Szyman stopped, standing amongst the field of black and white flowers. He turned away from Malaika, the mist surrounding him. "This is a good spot."

Malaika stepped back from Szyman, letting him find his footing in the field. He extended his palms and exhaled a single breath.

Around him, a city rose from the flowers. The streets poised a replica of a city in the country of Evylain, where Malaika had frequented over the years. With its brick pathways, stacked buildings, and hulking fortresses, it sprawled out in front of them like a soul released from the dead. Szyman reconstructed not just the vision of the city but its livelihood as well. While no one loitered in these misty streets, Malaika imagined the people bustling to the different temples and citadels.

Szyman joined her side. "I discovered I could do this years ago. Now, the Evylain army uses this skill to derail the Kainan opposition." He grinned. "It's unique and interesting, in a way. When I was younger, my friend Dee and I used to play games in my magical cities, pretending we were a king and queen... or sometimes just a baker and a patron. We had to stop when some stingy officials discovered us. They were not fond of that at all."

"Shame you couldn't keep up your games. Maybe someday you can invite this Dee out on the plains and show her here. I'm sure it would be fascinating."

"Dee is here with me now. She's my commander, Dame Dobroslawa Goryl."

"Oh, so you get to spend time with your *friend*, then?" Malaika continued to pry.

Szyman chuckled, "No, we're not like that. I do not have those sorts of feelings for anyone, really. Only friends... that's all."

Guess we're more similar than I thought. Malaika eyed the different structures fading into the surrounding mist. "So I'm guessing she has commanded you to do this?"

"Oh yes, many times. It derails Kainan when engaged in battle." Szyman continued grinning as he spoke. "They don't like magic in the slightest. But if they knew I could release souls like Moltod, then they might think a little differently."

"Moltod? Is that like your Kifo Kibaya?"

"Our God of Abstract and Death, yes." He ran his fingers through one of the misty structures, letting it collapse at his touch. "Although, I am unsure how this skill could benefit such a god."

"I guess you'll gotta wait until death to find out," Malaika remarked.

Szyman eyed her, "Wait. What do you mean?"

"As far as I know, all the Mist Keepers are dead. So I think that will happen to you too."

Malaika and Szyman walked back to the campsite in silence. Szyman kept his hands behind his back as he walked, attention focused on the horizon.

When they arrived at the campsite, Szyman ventured into one of the tents, leaving Malaika to sit alone by the fire. She kept the mist as a blanket, wrapping herself in it and hiding from wandering eyes. Even the confession she told Szyman left her with a strange emptiness. To be a Mist Keeper meant death; Malaika had never heard those words spoken, but it had to be true. Until she died, her magic hadn't come to fruition.

But... Szyman had his magic already. Did he need death to guide him?

There were so many things that Ningursu had never told her. Was it with reason? Or was it a mere oversight?

And why did Szyman enter the mist now? Weren't there supposed to be hundreds upon hundreds of years between each Mist Keeper?

Or... did others exist, loitering in the shadows?

She pulled her map forward, scanning the different countries and seas. The Mist Keepers remained scattered across the globe, never remaining in one place.

Other than, of course, Teodozia, sitting in her one spot, chained to the swamp.

Her heart ached as she stared at Teodozia. What would become of Szyman if he failed? What would become of her? Would Ningursu remold them in the image he so desired?

I can't... Malaika climbed to her feet, letting her map fall away as she turned toward the tents. Her head spun as she approached. *I must tell him.*

The tent opened. Szyman stepped out, wringing his hands together. "Oh, Malaika, I—"

Malaika interjected, "I can't let you do this."

"What?"

"Be a Mist Keeper. Or, at least, one of Ningursu's Mist Keepers. I can't let you do it." Malaika exhaled as she finished the sentence. "Please, understand. Ningursu... He does not like those who don't fit his idea. He turns them into monsters and—"

"Malaika, it's alright. I do not want to be a Mist Keeper as it is. Not if it means dying." Szyman glanced back into his tent, then out towards the Schanifeld. "I enjoy life far too much. Alive, we can change. In death, we are forced to reckon with our failures."

With a sigh, Malaika slumped onto the ground. "You're a wise man, Szyman. Wiser than me."

"I do not need my future mapped by some God of Abstract. I have my own path to follow."

"That is why I did not want you to join. Ningursu likes to be in control."

"Has he controlled you, though?"

"Not yet. And I hope, with all my prayers to Uzyma, that he never will."

Szyman sat on the ground beside her. In silence, they watched the mist rise and fall in the distance. In each passing beat, the questions of uncertainty lingered. What would happen to Szyman? And if Ningursu found out, what might he do to Malaika?

Nothing. He'll do nothing to me. Just like he has done nothing after all this time.

The world waited at her fingertips, and she was the only one who held its map.

THIRTY

After a fortnight, Szyman and his squadron abandoned their campsite in the Schanifeld, leaving Malaika behind as they disappeared on the horizon. Before leaving, Szyman told her to visit Freiborn at the edge of the Schanifeld.

"Dobroslawa is to marry her betrothed, so we must escort her back home," he said to her. "I'll be staying there for some time as a resource... so if you ever need anything, I will make sure there is a place for you."

"Thank you, Szyman, but you don't need to do that."

"I am your friend, Malaika. It is no trouble at all."

The words lingered as Szyman and his squadron departed. Their departure only signaled for Malaika to continue her adventure, back to releasing souls and searching out truths. She moved with intent, hopping between different cities and towns, saving souls with the knowledge of Szyman hid. Secrets, she knew now, loitered deep in the mist. There were things Ningursu would never tell her. Was it worth it to even ask?

Probably not, she realized. Ningursu did not put his faith in her. Why would he confide in her about the true nature of the mist?

As she ventured down the Eastern Continent, across the smoke-riddled mountains of Rosada, and into the swamps of Volfium, she weighed her options. What would she tell Ningursu when she arrived? What truth could she pull from him... if any at all?

She rehearsed different scenarios in her head. In one, she confronted Ningursu and demanded an answer. When he refused, she tossed him into the water, never to be seen again. In another, she threatened him, and he spilled the truths in fear. But one scenario beckoned for her like none other; the one where she did not come out victorious and instead fell to Ningursu's command. There, he captured her with his smoke-riddled chains, lacing her to the tree for all eternity.

That scenario seemed like the most likely outcome. Ningursu would not let his control fall.

So Malaika abandoned the idea of interrogation by the time she arrived in the swamp. Her new mission had rectified itself in her heart: truth. She would search far and wide for the undeniable truth of the situation. Ningursu might hide it, but the mist had the answers. If she mapped out the right questions, explored for the right answers, and gathered the right facts, then no secrets could hide from her.

She straightened her back, surrounding herself with determination as she stepped into the heart of the vermillion trees. The mud masked her footsteps, sloshing about her ankles. Teodozia's yellow smoke rippled around her, sending waves wreaking of sulfur and rotting flesh. Malaika held her breath as she stepped through the trees.

Then paused.

Aelia stood before Teodozia with an old jar in her hands. She kept her eyes locked on Teodozia. No one spoke.

Not Aelia.

Not Malaika.

Not Teodozia.

Aelia removed the lid from the jar.

A thick smoke, almost solid in nature, reached from the glass for Teodozia. The Diabolo winced as it surrounded her. It pulled at her skin, dismembering her piece by piece, leaving behind a trail of dust in the air. Aelia gathered the smoke and dust with a single wave, sending it back into the jar and fastening the lid.

Before Malaika could cry out, Aelia vanished into the mist.

THIRTY-ONE

Malaika summoned her map, locating Aelia as she traveled through the mist. At once, Malaika followed, summoning the mist as her pathway and moving only a few paces behind Aelia. What had happened to Teodozia? She couldn't be gone, right? And why did this happen now?

She reined in her thoughts, focusing on where mist guided her. She had to protect her friends.

Just like she protected Pam.

As she supported Jullian and Tabia.

And as she guided Szyman.

Today, it was Teodozia.

Malaika exited the mist into a thicker fog, belonging not to the dead but to the swamp itself. She barely made out Aelia's shadow moving through the trees, but she followed closely, maintaining her map as a guide and compass. The land beneath her feet steepened, the mud dissipating and replaced with firm soil. Aelia kept a steady pace, Malaika keeping a good minute behind her to not be seen.

The fog originated at the mouth of a cave, puffing like the smoke of a dragon. Aelia paused there, then stepped into the dark entrance, leaving Malaika outside the cave. If she stopped here, Aelia would never know her presence.

But once inside, her shield would fall.

She gulped once and stepped inside the cave.

The cave itself was nothing special. With dripping stalagmites and slippery floors, it would easily be a place that most would overlook. The path itself extended farther than Malaika could see, darkness in its purest form greeting her at the end. Malaika gulped once, checked her map, then let the mist once again pull her forward to where Aelia had stopped.

As if skidding on ice, she slid into the cave, grabbing onto her stone to keep her footing. Once the dizziness subsided, she took in her surroundings.

Shelves upon shelves lined the walls of the cave. Upon them stood rows of jars, yellow in tone, smudged and sealed.

Malaika lifted one from a nearby shelf and peered inside it. *What is this?*

After checking over her shoulder for Aelia, she opened the jar. A chartreuse, grotesque fog exploded from the top. It wreaked worse than the mist that had surrounded Teodozia, like a dead body decomposing right inside the jar.

The fog took shape, molding like clay before Malaika into an elongated, clawed hand. Before she could close the lid again, it reached forward and grabbed hold of her face.

She was lost.
Once again.
Lost.
Losing.
Alone.
No matter the map.
No matter the path.
It only took her back to the start.
Repeat...
    Repeat...
        Repeat...
No one beside her.
All others gone.
No one to loiter.

All souls passed beyond.

No one...

No one...

No one...

All at rest.

All at calm.

All at peace.

All but one.

Alone...

Alone...

Alone...

Alone.

"But I'm not alone!" She shouted. As tears fell from her cheeks and her head spun, she forced the lid of the jar closed, trapping the wicked hand inside its glass. Her heart pounded in her ears, but with the hand gone, the smoke subsided.

Alone, Malaika now stood in the rows of jars again. *These are all some sort of monster...*

Or...are they all Diabolos?

Footsteps caught her attention. She wiped her face, shoving the jar into her bag before Aelia discovered anything out of place.

THIRTY-TWO

"Hullo, Aelia," Malaika said as the woman emerged from between the shelves.

"Malaika!? What are you doing here? Why were you shouting?" Aelia asked. As always, despite a journey through the swamp and forest, her hair remained impeccable, and her blue dress pristine.

"To get your attention, of course!" Malaika chuckled, hiding her nerves. "Where's Teodozia?"

"What are you talking about?"

"I saw you. You trapped her in a jar!"

"I... did. Yes." Aelia laced her hands together, eyeing the shelving. She adjusted a few jars on the shelf, pausing the empty spot. "That wasn't Teodozia. Stealing that jar won't do you any good."

Malaika winced and cursed under her breath.

"Give it back. Now."

"Only if you tell me where Teodozia is and why you trapped her!" Malaika object.

"I shall. But give me back the jar first."

Malaika grunted, then reached into her bag. Her fingers trailed over the top of the monster's jar, then paused. Just beside it sat the empty jar of dye she had taken from home. She had almost forgotten about it, keeping it back in her hoarded collection of items. Willing her fingers to remain still, she lifted it from her bag. With its murky exterior and thick glass, it bore the exact resemblance to the jars on the shelves.

Aelia took it from her without question and placed it back in line with the other jars.

"Very good. Come."

Malaika glanced back once at the jar, then followed behind Aelia. They didn't speak as they lined the rows of shelves. Aelia didn't explain a thing, her attention unwavering. Malaika couldn't get a good understanding of Aelia, even after all these years. Her emotion turned to stone like her walk, like nothing more than a statue.

Is this what years of being Ningursu's subordinate do?

Aelia's stride halted in front of another unassuming shelf. She removed a jar and held it before Malaika. "Here is your Teodozia."

"How do I know you're not lying to me? All of these are the same. Show me her."

"No. But if you look in the jar, you'll see that it's her."

Malaika wrinkled her nose and eyed the jar. Nothing, at first, appeared different.

Then she saw it floating inside: a single piece of yarn.

"It is her…" Malaika whispered.

"Yes. A strand of yarn got caught while I was trapping her. I suppose it only makes sense for her to have that unique charm about her."

"And why is that?" Malaika asked, fixated on the jar still.

"She was the first… so it makes sense that she is indeed the last."

"The first Diabolo, you mean?"

"Yes, the first Diabolo I created. I wish she was the last, but…" Aelia sighed as she stared into the jar as well. "I will you this, Malaika. There was a war between the Council and other opposing forces, so Ningursu and I sought out more Mist Keepers. That was when I met my first apprentice, Teodozia. But…she didn't do well and ultimately succumbed to the mist. I tried to save her by injecting her with my concoction, made of the souls of the dead. It did not go as expected.

"But she was powerful in this form. She threatened our opponents. But our opponents had their own strengths as well. Magic is a chaotic tool when unleased. So we had to create more—one a year, with each of my failed apprentices." Her voice still did not quiver, no tears in her eyes as she spoke. "Seventy-nine Diabolo came before Tomás finally joined the Mist. After the war, as part of the treaty, we were instructed to destroy them. For years, we have tried to cure them, destroy them, abolish them...something. But we couldn't find a way. We imprisoned them in secret hiding places across the world that only Ningursu and I knew about, but we kept Teodozia close to watch how she grew over the years."

"But she has been getting more human!" Malaika interjected. "I've become her friend and—"

Aelia shook her head. "She is manipulating you, Malaika. She is not human. She will never be human again. Now that we have finally secured them, it is for everyone's safety that she is locked away."

"You're lying," Malaika spat. "You saw she was improving. You don't want her to learn how to speak! Because I am sure there are countless secrets she can spill about you and Ningursu and this dang Council!"

"It is not like that, Malaika. We had to secure her. And now we shall leave her." Aelia placed Teodozia's jar back on the shelf. "I'll give you a minute to say goodbye to your... *friend*. You will not have access here ever again."

Aelia walked over to the neighboring shelf, watching Malaika from the corner of her eye as she adjusted one of the jars.

Malaika held her bag close, holding back the tears as she pictured Teodozia rubbing the sweater against her face.

"Teodozia..." she murmured. "I promise, I'm here."

She eyed Aelia again. The woman had turned her back to dust another jar.

Malaika acted. She knocked Teodozia's jar into the bag and with a swift movement, placed the jar with the other Diabolo in its place.

Aelia turned just as she finished adjusting the jar. "Let us leave."

"Yes, Aelia. Of course," Malaika stared one last time at the jar. "Goodbye...Teodozia."

THIRTY-THREE

After Aelia led Malaika from the cave, the two parted without a mere word. Malaika wandered away from the blanket of white smoke and to higher ground, where pine trees towered, leaving a myriad of needles across the forest floor. She didn't look back, nor did she dare remove the jar from her bag.

Not yet. Not now. She clutched the strap of her bag, squinting into the late afternoon light. Once more, she would wander, build friendships, and explore every corner of the world. After all, this was her world to explore. Not Ningursu or the Council's world. They could stay in their fetid swamp for all she cared.

"I'm free," Malaika said to herself as she stepped out from between the trees. A green pasture waited for her. Cattle grazed, undisturbed by her presence. With Teodozia in her bag, nothing tethered her to the Council any longer. Why return when they saw her as a burden? From the beginning, she had been nothing more than an irksome little itch on the Council's scalp.

But she knew, as with every year, she would return to this swamp to report on her experiences. Malaika could not deny the bond she shared with the other Mist Keepers. She was part of their Council.

But their desires would not manipulate her.

She sat at the edge of the farm, staring out at the livestock and the dimming sky. After checking once at her map that no one had followed, she removed Teodozia's jar from the bag. She observed the glass, where the single strand of yarn lingered.

At least she brought her sweater with her. Malaika's hand gripped the lid of the jar. She twisted it.

Then stopped.

As much as she wanted to free Teodozia, it was too risky. She had to be sure that Teodozia would not escape... especially so close to the Council.

She held the jar up to the light. It swirled. "Teodozia... listen. We're going to find someplace safe. I've got friends that can help all over the world. We'll find someplace where you'll be free to be... you. But you have to stay in the jar just a bit longer, okay? Until I take us there. Do you understand?"

Nothing changed about the jar.

Malaika couldn't even be sure if Teodozia heard, let alone understood, her.

"I can at least keep you out of the bag. Here, I'll lace you to my belt. That way, you can see the world. I'm sure it's changed since you last left that swamp, huh?"

No response.

Malaika didn't expect one.

She slowly laced the jar to her belt, letting it rest against her leg. Then she leaned back, resting her head against the fence as the sun closed in on the horizon.

There, in the last gasp of light, a shadow rose above the sun. Malaika jumped to her feet and laughed.

The shadow expanded above the sun, like the wings of a dragon spreading out and taking flight.

Malaika laughed, readying to call out to her old friend.

But then the shadow vanished into the descending night, nothing more than a single gasp of hope and promise of freedom.

Or perhaps it was only a cloud.

The Story Collector's Almanac

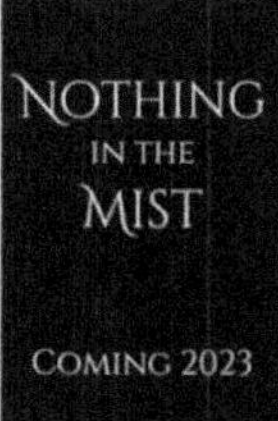

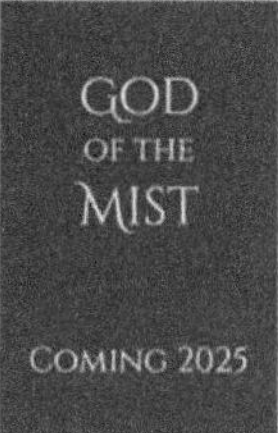

Also by E.S. Barrison...

Tales from the Effluvium
Speak Easy
These Sanguine Tides

The Unsought Fairytale Collection

Heims Norte
Kainan
Caligua
The Scr
(The Cloud)
The Indepen
City of Mer
Rosada
Volfium
Heims Sur
Proveniro
Perennes
Janis
Frin Ayl
Sichóu Shiyóu

Malaika's map of the world at the start of *The Mist Keeper's Apprentice*.

AUTHOR'S NOTE

Thank you so much for taking the time to read *Mapping the Mist*.

If you enjoyed this book, I would appreciate it if you could:

Review this book. Reviews are a great help to an author. If you enjoyed this book, please consider leaving a review online.

Tell Others. When you share this book with others on social media, you're allowing others to discover this story. Word-of-mouth is one of the best sources of marketing for an author.

Connect with me. If you want to find out about my upcoming releases, stop by my website at www.esbarrison-author.com or connect with me on social media.

Thank you!

E.S. Barrison

ACKNOWLEDGMENTS

To all the following, my thanks, for your support throughout this process:

First to Moira, my cover artist, for capturing Malaika perfectly for this cover.

To Charlie, my editor, for all your kindness and support in capturing Malaika's tale.

To Matthew, for letting me ramble whenever necessary.

And finally, to my readers, I hope you enjoyed this little adventure.

Without all your support, this story may never have come together as I intended.

ABOUT THE AUTHOR

E.S. Barrison has been writing and creating stories for as long as she can remember. After graduating from the University of Florida, she has spent the past few years wrangling her experiences to compose unique worlds with diverse characters. Currently, E.S. lives in Orlando, Florida with her family.